THE
LOVE CURSE
OF THE
RUMBAUGHS

BY JACK GANTOS

Heads or Tails: Stories from the Sixth Grade

Jack's New Power: Stories from a Caribbean Year

Desire Lines

Jack's Black Book

Joey Pigza Swallowed the Key

Jack on the Tracks: Four Seasons of Fifth Grade

Joey Pigza Loses Control

Hole in My Life

What Would Joey Do?

Jack Adrift: Fourth Grade without a Clue

The Love Curse of the Rumbaughs

THE
LOVE CURSE
OF THE
RUMBAUGHS

JACK GANTOS

FARRAR, STRAUS AND GIROUX

NEW YORK

Distributed in Canada by Douglas & McIntyre Ltd.
Printed in the United States of America
Designed by Robbin Gourley and Vera Soki
First edition, 2006
1   3   5   7   9   10   8   6   4   2

www.fsgkidsbooks.com

Library of Congress Cataloging-in-Publication Data
Gantos, Jack.
   The love curse of the Rumbaughs / Jack Gantos.— 1st ed.
      p.   cm.
   Summary: A young woman named Ivy, who made a shocking
discovery in her small western Pennsylvania town when she was
seven years old and learned a surprising secret nine years later,
questions whether she has inherited the Rumbaugh curse of having
excessive love for one's mother.
   ISBN-13: 978-0-374-33690-5
   ISBN-10: 0-374-33690-3
   [1. Mothers—Fiction.   2. Twins—Fiction.   3. Secrets—Fiction.
4. Taxidermy—Fiction.   5. Horror stories.]

PZ7.G15334Lov 2006
[Fic]—dc22

                                                           2005040124

*The author would like to thank the Boston Athenaeum for its
generous support during the writing of this book.*

For Anne and Mabel

THE
LOVE CURSE
OF THE
RUMBAUGHS

AN INTRODUCTION

I expect you might think the story I am about to tell you is untrue or perversely gothic in some unhealthy way. You might even think I've exaggerated the facts in order to twist this book into a modern-day metaphor on the exploitation of human creation, as did Mary Shelley with *Frankenstein*. Maybe you'll think I'm trying to spook you with a psychological tale of a murderous double as Edgar Allan Poe wrote in "William Wilson," or stir up family shame as Hawthorne did in *The House of the Seven Gables*. But my story is entirely different.

These gothic authors believed disturbing truths about deviant human behavior could only be revealed in settings that were slanted against nature. And although the literature is exceptional, the authors were only guessing at the dark side of the human condition because they based their books on superstition, not science.

But I don't need outdated gothic conventions with their weird characters, paranormal fallacies, and eerie locations in order to report what I know about human behavior. I am simply going to tell you a plain and true small-town story about a family love curse that is so passionate and so genuinely expressed that it transcends everything commonly accepted about how love reveals itself—or conceals itself. What I discovered about my family opened my eyes to how love, when nurtured behind closed doors, is capable of turning a forbidden obsession into something that seems so natural.

What I had first judged unsympathetically to be the primitive behavior of two ailing minds became an activity so comforting that after a while I couldn't understand why every family wouldn't consider it a time-honored tradition. Some people think the Rumbaugh love is a hereditary curse passed down from one tainted generation to the next, but I believe our family legacy is a compassionate gift.

I expect upon reading this book most people will disagree with my point of view and especially with my contribution to the curse. This is understandable. And even though I firmly believe I am in the right and have behaved reverently, my mother always said that Roman law reads: *In propria causa nemo judex*, "No one can be judge in his own cause." So for this story I'll give you the facts as I know them and leave it in your hands to pass judgment.

1
CURSED

In the presence of extraordinary actuality, consciousness takes the place of imagination.
—Wallace Stevens

THE TWINS

I am a young woman now, but when I was seven years old something unexpected happened that changed my life forever. It was Easter Sunday when a dramatic manifestation of the Rumbaugh curse was revealed to me. I found Abner and Adolph Rumbaugh's dead mother—for the first time—and it left the greatest impression.

Abner and Adolph were identical twins, and they grew more and more alike as they got older. There was no simple way to tell them apart, and after years of trying people gave up. Even when one brother was alone shopping along Main Street in our small western Pennsylvania town, people greeted him as "the Twins."

"How are the Twins?" a shopkeeper might ask the one who entered his store.

"We are fine," the single Twin would reply, perfectly comfortable to be both himself and his brother.

They were already old when I was born, and for as long as I remember I had thought they were living pieces of history, like the smoky, bug-specked photographs of Civil War soldiers lining the halls in the Westmoreland County Courthouse.

Everything about the Twins aged in a singular way, so that they stood out among other men as if they were an idiosyncratic variation within a breed, like cats with extra toes, or albino birds with see-through feathers. The Twins' waxy white hair was horsetail thick and glazed with the dirty gold color of old teeth and tobacco, and their thin, nearly transparent skin looked like milk spilled over a road map of blue and red veins. They were pharmacists, and I've never seen hands as clean as theirs, which they hygienically scrubbed to a ruddy glow at the beginning and end of each workday with a strong boar's hair nailbrush dipped in a shallow dish of coarse salt. When I asked if it hurt to scrub his hands, Ab (or it could have been Dolph) replied as if his words were a medical college oath he had pledged to uphold, "Good health is built on the foundation of a sanitary science." He held his hands erect before him as if he were drying two white-hot flames.

Nothing they did ever seemed accidental or whimsical, and pain or difficulty never stopped them from being thorough. You could always find some sense of purpose in their fixed eyes, which were as blue as the Dresden blue porcelain drawer pulls their mother had bought them for a gift after they graduated from pharmacy school in 1944. Once they returned home to Mount Pleasant from the University of Pittsburgh, they established their own business and worked diligently to keep up with the steady flow of Frick Hospital prescriptions and local clientele. It was only imprecision brought on by exhaustion that sent them down into their basement workshop to relax. Like many men in fish-and-game towns, they practiced taxidermy as a hobby. The Twins competed in contests at the Westmoreland County Fair and as far east as the county fairs in York and Lancaster and north up to Beaver Falls and Erie.

It was with great pride that within the pharmacy they displayed their winning entries in dust-proof glass-and-oak cases set on top of the tall shelves. In order that their handiwork be viewed more clearly, Ab and Dolph shimmed the back legs of the cases so they tilted downward for everyone to see. There was a set of squirrel pharmacists grinding medications with a mortar and pestle. There were conjoined pigs dressed in black suits, which they titled CHANG AND ENG after the famous Siamese twins. Another pair of Siamese twins—kittens this time—were titled THE HILTON SISTERS after Daisy and Violet Hilton. One kitten wore a blond wig, the other a brunette, and they were posed in tiny wedding gowns after a scene from the movie poster advertising their biographical film, *Chained for Life*. In another case a white mink slept on a little tufted bed while a black mink hovered above him. Below the scene was written: "I could not love except where Death was mingling *his* with Beauty's breath.—E. A. Poe."

There were dozens more, many decorated with blue and red prize ribbons and some with brassy shoulder braids like on an army general. I especially liked the long case that was labeled in gold script across the bottom of the frame THE RUMBAUGH BROOD—FITTER FAMILY CONTEST WINNER. In it was a father mink, a mother mink, and a dozen mink children in descending stair-step order, with all of them standing straight up in healthy muscleman poses except for the mother. She was cradling twin mink babies in her arms. Beneath each mink was a name, but I always skipped over them and read just the Twins' names, ADOLPH AND ABNER (*PERFECT TWINS*), because it made me smile warmly to think of them as cute little minks. Across the top of the frame was printed EUGENIC HEALTH EXHIBIT—WESTMORELAND COUNTY FAIR, 1921. Hanging from the corner was a gold medal kept in full shine with the image of parents reaching for a plump, smiling child, who in turn was reaching for them. Circling the family were the words "Yea, I Have a Goodly Heritage."

The Twins' father, Peter Rumbaugh, who was a mink farmer and taxidermist, had made the display for the Westmoreland Chapter of the Eugenics Research Association after the Rumbaugh family was awarded the Fitter Family Medal. He practiced taxidermy on minks from his mink farm, and the Twins, before he signed them over for adoption to the Eugenics Research Association, must have watched him. He even made them baby toys of stuffed animals on wheels—also on display—little minks and squirrels and chickens with metal loops through their noses and beaks to which leather pull cords were attached. Many years later he sent the Twins the pull toys and family mink exhibit in an attempt to reconcile their ruined relationship—which I will explain later. But no gesture could assuage their feeling that he had betrayed them. Besides, their mother, Mrs. Rumbaugh, with whom the Twins lived, steadfastly forbade the mention of his name.

As a child I stood on a step stool for hours and studied the various displays and creatures, admiring their fixed postures and expressions, the meticulously painted backgrounds, and especially their tiny clothes which the Twins had sewn with the help of their mother. She was good with her hands and made extra money by braiding elaborate mourning jewelry from the long hairs of the dead.

Despite their peculiar activities, the Twins always presented themselves very earnestly to the world. They wore identical black boiled-wool three-piece suits, each with a collarless white shirt which was fastened at the top with a single copper stud the size of a tack head. They wore the same shirts all week, so that circles of green oxidation edged the white buttonholes where the studs pressed just below their Adam's apples. On Sundays they wore the same suits, with freshly laundered and starched collared shirts and black ribbon bow ties. They were thin necked—"pencil necked" my mother called them—but because of their age both had identical wattles of ruddy chicken skin gathered over the collars of their shirts. When they spoke they pecked at the air as if the words were grains of corn, and their wattles flopped about like deflated balloons.

For some inexplicable reason, unknown to me when I was young, I was born deeply in love with the Twins. I adored them so much it hurt to see their physical flaws because I wanted them to be perfect in the way you wish a drawing to appear on paper as precisely as you saw it in your mind. I wished I could have taken a small scissors and snipped off the extra folds of skin and finely sewn the necks back together and smoothed the scars with lanolin. I knew even then it could not have been difficult to do so.

On that astonishing Easter morning, my mother and I had worn matching yellow dresses with wide white patent-leather belts pulled tightly round our waists. We wore identical yellow satin headbands with our black hair pushed back behind our ears and our bangs combed forward to just above our dark eyebrows. She wore red lipstick, and after she kissed me on the lips we examined ourselves in the mirror and I was very pleased to see that my lips were red, too. "Mom and mini-Mom" we called ourselves as we left the Kelly Hotel and walked in our black patent-leather shoes down Diamond Street toward the Transfiguration Polish Catholic Church. It was a warm sunny day and I was very happy.

Easter Mass is always a festive service at T.P.C.C., with potted lilies lining the central aisle at every oak pew. Their white blossoms were pointed toward the altar, where the glowing monstrance stood like a golden lighthouse. The sacred body of Christ beamed out through that glass eye as mysteriously as a holy Cyclops. Along the walls polite arrangements of carnations graced the feet of the apostles and saints. But an early spring garden of vibrant flowers framed the stained-glass window that pictured a trapped coal miner kneeling in prayer before the image of the Virgin Mary. The older ladies in black dresses may have lost husbands, brothers, and sons in the local coal mines, yet they never lost hope that the buried would someday emerge from the ground like Lazarus, a miracle to behold. Once, a coal tunnel dug by mistake under the edge of town caved in. Above it, buildings staggered, then toppled. Trees slipped down holes like vanishing scarves in a magic trick. The older ladies gathered on the banks of the open trench, calling out names, hoping their lost men might be alive like the French troops who had been trapped in their elaborate tunnels during World War II, only to surface years later, blinking and pale as grubs.

After Father Baumann led us in prayer, he pointed out how the trumpet-shaped lily blossoms announced the good news of salvation. Then he transfixed me with the story of how Jesus had been fitted with the crown of thorns, nailed to the rugged cross He had been savagely beaten to carry, then pierced with a spear and left to bleed to death. He was laid to rest in the cool stone tomb and later came back from the dead and wandered about, convincing Doubting Thomas and performing various miracles, before ascending on a gilded cloud toward the blue curtain of the sky, where God and the Holy Spirit and a chorus of angels in shimmering robes reached out to greet Him.

This all created a beautifully staged pageant in my mind and had me thinking about coming back from the dead and what that might mean. Could you come back all healed? Would you remember who you were? Would you remember where you had been while dead? Or was there no coming back for us regular people? Was death for us just a stone hole of lonely black air where there was no difference between keeping your eyes open and keeping them closed?

I had turned toward my mother to whisper these questions in her ear when I saw she was crying. Her open eyes were like shards of ice melting. Suddenly a strong feeling flooded my heart with as much power and clarity as any thought which had ever entered my mind. I *knew* she was feeling what Mary had felt. While everyone in Jerusalem was looking up to heaven and praising God, Mary was weeping inside her child's empty tomb. How could Jesus endure leaving her behind, I wondered, when just the thought of leaving my mother for a moment was unbearable? He preferred the glory of heaven above, but I preferred my beautiful mother, who was heaven on earth.

I slid my hand across the pew and held hers, which was always as warm and soft as the inside of fresh bread. I waited until we were outside before I asked the question on my mind. "If you die first, would you come back from the dead if you could?"

"Ivy Spirco, if I could look halfway decent and not moldy like Lazarus, who was more of a zombie, I will. Otherwise," she said without melancholy, "I'll just stretch out on a nice cumulus cloud and wait for you."

"And what if I die first?" I asked.

She waved off the question. "God forbid," she said, then before I could hang on her coat sleeve and tug more talk out of her, Ab and Dolph swung forward and blocked our path like a set of identical doors.

They belonged to the German Lutheran church up on Main Street. My mother had told me that the difference between the Catholics and the Lutherans was that when Catholics got out of church they were more relieved than when they entered, and when Lutherans got out of church they were more worried. Neither seemed right to me. I always wanted to stay in church and imagine my mother and me in heaven, dressed as tiny brides and living side by side in towering wedding-cake houses.

"Excuse me," one of the Twins said, snapping to attention.

"Would you care to retire to the pharmacy for some Easter refreshments?" the other enunciated, speaking precisely, as if he were adding up numbers rather than asking a simple question.

They were very odd talkers, because when they spoke in public their thoughts lashed out like military announcements, and when they spoke in private conversation, they only whispered like conspirators hatching a plot. But I was used to them because every day I spent a few hours at the pharmacy between when I got out of school and when Mom's bus pulled in from Greensburg, where she worked as a courtroom stenographer.

"Let's go," I said to Mom, and squeezed her hand as if

spurring a horse. We had plans to have Easter lunch at the Kelly Hotel dining room, but we still had time for refreshments. Besides, the Twins kept cold drinks and tubs of ice cream behind their gray marble and pleated chrome soda counter, and I had given up ice cream for Lent and was eager for a bowlful.

Mom glanced at her watch. "We'd love to," she replied, then reached out to brush something that looked like sawdust off Ab's or Dolph's coat sleeve. "Termites?" she asked playfully.

He looked horrified and awkwardly jerked away from her, then slapped at his sleeve as if it were on fire. "It's nothing," he said nervously. "Nothing at all."

It was something, but I was too fixated on ice cream at the time to care about a little sawdust. "Let's go," I said, and hauled Mom forward. As she passed the Twins she gripped Ab's or Dolph's hand and he grabbed his brother's. They were slow walkers when they had to follow, and they were speed walkers when they led.

"Come on, Ab," she said as if coaxing a donkey. "Pick it up, Dolph."

I could never tell one from the other so seldom chanced any name and stuck with pronouns, but Mom never cared if she had gotten their names right. When I was younger I thought she possessed psychic powers for telling them apart, but as I grew older I realized the Twins simply adjusted to whichever name she gave them. They were as interchangeable to each other as they were to us. They told me that themselves.

"You heard her," Dolph snapped at Ab. "Don't be slow-footed."

"Don't you be, neither," Ab said curtly, and clenched his jaw.

"Now, boys," Mom said, and she yanked again on Dolph's hand and in turn he yanked on Ab's and we tacked down the brick sidewalk all leaning forward as if battling headwinds.

They were seventy-one years old.

I broke my Lenten fast with three scoops of chocolate ice cream in a white glass sundae dish that was the shape of an eyewash cup. I ate quickly because I had something else on my mind. Something thrilling. In the basement I had my special after-school play area, which I called the Rabbit's Hideaway because the floor was matted with different colors of shredded cellophane like Easter basket grass. The cellophane had been used as packing for the drug shipments, and the Twins saved it for me and made a quaint peaceable kingdom of small taxidermed black-and-white rabbits and kittens and foxes for me to play with.

They also set aside the oversize display products they never bothered to use in their windows. I had an aspirin box the size of a refrigerator, which I called my cottage. Inside it I had two giant Ivory soap bars, which had been carved out of dense foam. They were my guest chairs. I had an inflatable thermometer the size of a baseball bat and a giant Dr. Scholl's foot pad, which I rolled out and used as a carpet. In my kitchen corner I had a six-pack of inflatable Coke bottles, a large box of Arm & Hammer baking soda, and a colorful assortment of empty pillboxes and medicine bottles donated by the Twins. Along the edge of my cottage property, tall black plastic tubes of pointy lipstick stood in a fence row. This was my private play world where I spent most of my time after school, and I loved it.

Ab and Dolph would regularly scratch down the stone stairs in their broad leather wingtips and check up on me, or bring me ice cream bars and lemonade. They also had a drug room down there that was a strong walk-in wire cage, where they stored all the expensive drugs and the drugs that would most likely be stolen by addicts. They had it built after a burglar broke into the upstairs drug closet. Often, one of them was in the basement sorting through boxes and keeping me silent company while I played.

On that Easter Sunday, after I finished my ice cream, it got into my mind that the Twins may have set up an Easter egg hunt in my hideaway. It was like them to do sweet little things for me.

"May I go to the bathroom?" I asked Ab, fishing for the excuse I needed to go downstairs. By then Mom had gotten tired of saying *boys* and had taken a marker and drawn a big *A* on Ab's hand and a *D* on Dolph's.

"No," Mom quickly said before Ab could get his mouth in motion. "Not now, we'll be leaving in a minute."

Then she abruptly pointed up at the sky. "Look," she cried to the Twins as she pointed out the window, "you can make out a blue highway in the sky. It's a zonal jet stream cutting though a layer of heavy air." The Twins squinted so intensely they were cross-eyed from trying to locate some distant artery of blueness beyond the tip of her finger.

I looked out the window, too—but not at the weather. Across the street was the red brick and white trim of the Kelly Hotel, where we lived. On the ground floor was the Kelly Tavern, and on the sidewalk hulking, round-shouldered men, old coal miners and farmers mostly, in baggy dark suits and white shirts, had lined up outside the tavern side door like a row of empty bottles. The coal miners squinted and blinked under the bright sun. The farmers paced back and forth as if plowing rows. The tavern, by tradition, only served once the church bells stopped, and Father Baumann, who was animated with the Easter spirit, was ringing our Transfiguration Church bells as if he were attempting to wake the dead.

"Look at how they are celebrating the end of Lent," Adolph commented disapprovingly toward the men who shifted impatiently from foot to foot.

"Every day is the end of Lent for them that drinks," Ab pronounced as he rubbed his eyes.

"Now, now," my mother said. "The Kellys are a nice family. They just serve a different medicine than you do."

"Better off drinking formaldehyde," Ab said without mercy.

"Be embalmed before they die," added Dolph.

"Well, if you worked in the mines or fields," my mother ventured, "you'd need something to fortify your wits."

" 'When the wine is in, the wit is out,' " Dolph quoted, wagging a long, disapproving finger toward the men.

"Besides, we entertained mining," Ab said. "We had a summer of it before going to the university."

"Mother didn't approve," Dolph whispered. "Said it was too dangerous. Would walk us to the shaft over at Mutual and be there when the lift brung us up. Said her days above the ground waiting for us were darker than our days under it."

My mother nodded. She didn't have much to say when Mrs. Rumbaugh's name came up. Mom belonged to the school of manners where you didn't say anything if you didn't have anything good to say, and she had known Mrs. Rumbaugh and so kept her mind to herself. Even at such a young age I knew some of the reasons why she held her tongue.

When Mom was fifteen, Mrs. Rumbaugh hired her to work in the pharmacy. Part of her job was to stock and manage the section dedicated to women's sanitary products. Mrs. Rumbaugh, who worked the register, had wanted to hire an older woman for the position, knowing that it was easier for women to take advice regarding intimate issues from a more matronly lady. But there was no self-respecting older lady in Mount Pleasant who would take the job, and Mrs. Rumbaugh was uncomfortable doing it herself. A woman's personal needs were just too delicate a subject to be associated with in such a small, talkative town. Until my mother was hired, the only women's sanitary products were located in the back corner of the store. The Twins just kept an open box of Tampax and Kotex and discreet little waxed brown paper bags on a shelf, and women could take what they needed without having to pay. The boys never charged for this convenience and averted their eyes whenever a woman drifted toward the dimly lit corner. But after the new Rexall drugstore aggressively moved in up the street, Mrs. Rumbaugh knew they were losing customers and money by not promoting a full range of sanitary and birth-control items. She hired Mom to help customers with their most personal needs. Mom had a quick way of putting people at their ease, which helped because some of the women were squeamish, and with the men she could use her sense of humor.

Years later, when I was old enough to understand, Mom impishly told me, "When a man asked me for prophylactics, I'd always ask him what size he needed. The stumped look that froze their faces liked to kill me. It's one of the few joys I took from the job."

Even though Mrs. Rumbaugh hired Mom and must have seen what a valuable employee she turned out to be, she was not pleasant toward her.

"Their mother wasn't nice to anyone unless she was steering them to do something for her," Mom said on more than one of her anti-Rumbaugh rants. "She was like all the other Rumbaughs, always driven by purpose. Never pleasure. For her, being nice was a tool to get what she wanted. I could look into her eyes on the few times she was being decent to me, and I could tell that she was not feeling nice inside. She was always scheming. And those boys couldn't make a move without her breathing down their necks. She wouldn't let them talk to me.

No wonder they never married. Not allowed to look at a woman. No fun allowed. Never went to the movies, or out to dinner. They never went to a ball game in Pittsburgh or played pool or bowled or were allowed to do anything that she or their church didn't sanction. The more overbearing she was the more obedient they were. If I wasn't such a good girl I would've found a way to spoil her grip."

Mom also took over the cosmetics buying, updating and expanding the selection. This addition to the store became popular with schoolgirls, and before long Mom was responsible for a rich stream of store revenue.

"The more successful I was the more she resented me," Mom said. "If it hadn't been for the boys, I never would have stayed. They treated me sweetly when she wasn't around. A kind word to them and they'd blush for hours. One kiss and they'd eat out of my hands. They were stunted, like emotional dwarves. I see a lot of their type in court. Eventually they snap, and look out when they do."

By the time Mom did find a way to warm up the Twins, Mrs. Rumbaugh was dead, but her grip wasn't entirely loosened. Their mother had more influence over them than even she knew.

After we had spent a long time looking out the pharmacy window and watching the Lent-breaking men eagerly rush into the tavern, I *needed* the bathroom.

"But I have to go," I said in a whiny voice. "I'll be fast."

"Just as far as the bathroom," Ab said, fidgeting about with his raw hands.

"No farther," echoed Dolph. "No playing in your cottage today. The light's out back there."

But I didn't listen to them. I knew they had something hidden down there for me. Their warning only seemed to be part of a game, so I stood up, opened the basement door, and inched carefully down the dark, granite stairs.

If on that Easter Sunday I had found one of the Twins dead in the basement of their Rumbaugh Pharmacy, I would have been startled but not puzzled. Even at the age of seven I knew it was the nature of things to grow old and die. I accepted that without question in the way farmers around here anticipate the life and death of their crops, or the way miners trade their wages for half a life. However, their mother had been dead for eight years and should have been deep in the grave and not deep in the basement, where I found her standing stiffly in front of me, one arm by her side and the other reaching out with a dark, waxy little hand, like a monkey paw.

I had used the toilet and was smoothing out the full skirt on my Easter dress as I carefully stepped toward my cottage in the dark back corner. The lights down there were dim but not out, as the Twins had warned, and when I first saw the mother I thought it was an old dressmaker's mannequin, like the kind I had seen in secondhand shops. As I got closer, it seemed to be more of a large doll because it had a head. I looked at the face, which was the color of a paper bag. It was crumpled up a bit from dryness, and if I had known it was their mother I would have screamed. But because I thought it was a doll I looked at it more carefully, as though I'd found a treasure among the basement clutter of old Bavarian furniture and moldy leather trunks and crates from when the first Rumbaughs immigrated to western Pennsylvania from Germany before the Civil War.

The doll was wearing a long black satin dress with an elaborately knotted shawl, like a thick black spider's web draped around her shoulders. I noticed a gold wedding band on one of her fingers and when I reached out and touched it, she rolled back a bit, and I saw she was mounted on an oval piece of wood painted to look like a little braided hearth rug. There was something familiar and kindhearted about the painted rug which made me feel at ease. I knelt down and peeked under the wood and saw four small hard plastic wheels, like the kind you find on the legs of a sofa that swivels about. That's when I saw her shoes. She was a fancy doll, I supposed, and I became even more curious as I still collected and played with dolls, gave them names, and slipped eagerly into their busy worlds. The shoes were tiny, cramped-looking black lace-up half boots, just like the ones all the old European ladies wore to church. I reached out and touched the toe of one shoe and ran my fingertips up the metal eyelets as if practicing scales on a flute.

That's when I noticed there was a small space between the frayed hem of the dress and the top rim of the shoe, just above the knotted lace. I lifted the hem. The stale air trapped beneath the dress smelled like mothballs. I shivered and turned my head away for a breath of fresh air. I knew I shouldn't go any farther, but I couldn't stop myself. I turned back and raised the dress even higher. Her thick legs were covered with black cotton stockings, but the seam on one of the stockings was ripped along the side.

I moved just a little closer and with both hands pulled open the seam so I could examine the leg. It was made out of leather, I thought, and was dark brown and split open like a puffy old baseball glove. With my finger I poked at the tear in the tanned leather and a small piece cracked off. A spoonful of sawdust spilled out and gathered in a tiny mound around her heel. I jerked my hand away.

I was aware that a lot of time had passed, so I stood up and backed away, and as I did I looked up at her face again. Her lips were the color of tarnished pennies. They were sealed tightly, and stitched up at the corners to give her a bit of a smile. It was impossible to know what she was smiling about because her large brown eyes were fixed in a glassy, straight-forward way that I had seen only in stuffed deer heads. Those eyes were empty of life yet full of little sparks of trapped light, like a candlewick still glowing once the flame has been blown out.

My mother had always said that when you look straight into the eyes of a person you should be able to see directly into their soul, and if you see nothing, be wary. I still didn't know what I was looking at, but something inside me said to back away, to listen to my mother, and to be very, very careful. As I retreated, the basement shadows draped over her, yet through them I could still see those dead eyes glowing. Goose bumps flared up and down my legs. I kept stepping back, all along staring intently at her ridged face and at that waxy little monkey paw, which I expected to uncoil and snatch me by the chin.

Then, at the moment my heart began to race from fear, I realized I had seen that taut, determined face before. I was certain. Suddenly it came over me that she was Ab and Dolph's mother, because she looked exactly like the large sepia-toned photograph they had of her in their upstairs office. It was the same dress, and same creepy shawl, and same "secret" smile. This was all churning roughly in my mind, and I turned away as if looking in another direction might erase what I had discovered. And then some impulse jerked me back around and I looked at her again. I had to be sure of what I saw before I said anything upstairs. At that moment one of the little wheels shifted, and she abruptly tipped forward.

I was too frightened to scream as I clambered up the stone stairs. Halfway up, my feet slipped out beneath me and I pitched forward onto my hands and knees. I continued to scramble upward on all fours, mute with fear until I reached the last step and pushed the heavy basement door, which opened directly into the store. I hopped up and let out an animal wail that froze my mother and the Twins, and then the three of them leapt toward me.

"What is it?" my mother asked, and hoisted me up into her arms. As she did so, she glanced crossly at Ab and Dolph for a fraction of a second before turning back toward me. At the time I gave no thought to her flashing, stern expression, but when I think back on it I realize she knew immediately what I had seen and she was angry with them for being so careless.

"The bear," Dolph said nervously toward his brother, and marched past me to latch the door.

Ab cleared his throat. "Bear," he repeated, then turned toward my mother. "An old stuffed bear," he said stiffly. "It's being sent out for repair."

"That's not a bear," I said, heaving myself out of a sob. "It was your mother."

"Honey," Mom said, "you must have imagined it."

"No," I insisted, still crying between the gushes of words. From where my mother was holding me and fussing with my knees and hands I looked across the store and saw Mrs. Rumbaugh's portrait hanging in the back of the pharmacy. "It's her!" I wailed, pointing and boosting myself up over my mother's shoulder. "*She's* in the basement."

They all spun around and stared intently toward the portrait.

"Bear," Dolph said, nervously plucking at his neck skin. "It was the bear. It fell over and cracked its leg."

"It's dark down there," Ab said. "The light's puzzling."

"It's no bear," I persisted from fear and now fury. "It's wearing a dress and shoes!"

After I said that, an abrupt cushion of time seemed to smother us, and we all stood there as if unable to breathe. Cars passed. The phone rang. The wind blew and a door slammed in the distance, followed by the screech of a stuck window opening. Steam buckled a radiator. Early spring wasps tapped against the glass picture window. A lone cloud drifted in front of the sun like an eye patch. The stained-glass poppies in the transom window dimmed from bright yellow to dull gold, flickered, then brightened as the cloud moved on. A Greyhound bus pulled up to the sidewalk bench in front of the store, and the sudden hydraulic hiss of the brakes and folded doors slapping open brought us around.

"I think we better leave," Mom said through the still air. I had my legs clamped around her waist and chin dug into her neck as she turned, grabbed her purse, and staggered on her first step toward the door.

I was too much for her to carry, but there was nowhere else I wanted to be except wrapped around her and I knew she understood. I stared into Ab's and Dolph's fretful eyes and looked into their souls as Mom taught me, and I saw they were terrified. Dolph was slowly rubbing his hands over his face as if carefully wiping away cobwebs. Ab's head burrowed into his hunched shoulders, and he looked as grim and mold-stained as a weathered tree stump. It *was* their mother. And because I knew I was right, I had a surge of bravery.

"Do you want to see it?" I whispered in Mom's ear. "So you know I'm not lying."

"I know you aren't lying," she whispered back. And then, just to put Ab and Dolph at ease, she straightened her smile, turned back toward them, and said in a charming, reassuring voice, "Don't worry, boys. She's just a little tired, is all." She tucked a black curl behind her ear, and we left them standing as mute and helpless as the stuffed little minks in their mink mother's arms.

Now, twelve years later, as I sit in the Kelly Hotel, looking out our window and recalling that day, I see it was extraordinary in many ways. I found in that basement a certain symmetry of emotions—a balance between what is alluring and what is repulsive, and this pair of responses seemed to bookend the range of all my future emotions, especially my twin responses to Ab and Dolph, whom I could love dearly and hate passionately.

But even more significantly, it was a day in which who I truly was on the inside began to steer how I behaved on the outside. Without a sound, the Rumbaugh blood coursing through my veins was already charting my destiny, and I was just at the beginning of a journey dominated by a curse that would double back to capture me.

THE CALLING

There was no bear in the basement. It was their mother, and I wish they had told me the truth. If they had just tugged nervously on their wattles and stammered as they do and simultaneously admitted that it was their mother and that they couldn't stand to live without her and had lovingly preserved her so she would live with them forever, then I would have understood. To me it would have seemed tender of them, even normal, because without realizing it I was inflicted with the same mother fixation, even though I didn't know entirely what it was. Like any seven-year-old, I never wanted my mother to die. In a broad way I knew she would die someday, but that someday seemed so distant that it had no real power over me.

Anyway, I just wish Ab and Dolph had managed to tell me it was their mother and explain exactly what they had done to her, because without the facts, my imagination ran wild with what I had just seen in the basement.

At T.P.C.C. parochial school, Sister Nancy said I had been blessed with an infinite capacity for prayer because during quiet reading she observed I was content to reread the same Bible page over and over. One day she silently hovered above me for several minutes. Her billowing presence was like a cloud in the shape of a person. I put my finger next to the last sentence I'd read and glanced upward. With her face leaning over me her white fleshy cheeks were soft and plump as marshmallows. She looked me directly in the eye and nodded reverently. "I see you have the sacred gift of focus," she whispered. Her rosewood crucifix swung before me like a hypnotizing pendulum.

"How do you mean?" I asked.

She always knew in advance the answers to her questions. Only the truth would fail to disappoint her.

"You can read the same page over and over and find in it a deeper meaning each time. Is this true?" she asked.

Her face was so neutral that even if I lied to win her favor I still wouldn't know to agree or disagree with her.

"Yes, Sister," I said, pleased with the fullness of her attention. "After a while I can begin to read between the words, between the lines, and before long I can imagine an entirely different story based on one page."

"When I was your age, I learned that the faith of the saints was made infinite through imagination," she said. "I have come to understand that a prayer repeated results in countless meanings, and those meanings are united through the conviction of faith."

I understood Sister Nancy entirely. True devotion was the result of including all thoughts while excluding none, which is why even after my mother and I had left the pharmacy, the image of the Twins' mother continued to loop swiftly through my mind like a page repeated this way and that, obsessively modified as if I were styling a doll that had an endless wardrobe of accessories.

I could imagine Mrs. Rumbaugh from all angles—front to back, top to bottom, and with each pose I imagined her German accent calling out: *Love me, honor me, obey me, keep me alive in your hearts, and I will never abandon you at your time of need.* Even in death she commanded her sons, and in my imagination she now commanded me. She did not want to be forgotten, and I knew I would always remember our meeting because a Rumbaugh switch had been turned on within me and from that moment it could not be turned off.

"Are you *sure* you saw Mrs. Rumbaugh?" my mother asked on that Easter Sunday as we scurried home from the pharmacy.

"Yes," I said impatiently.

"Did you see more than one?"

Honestly, I didn't understand just how suggestive the question was, nor did I have any patience to consider it at the time. I was still a kid, and the moment Mom set me down feetfirst on the sidewalk, I began to race up Main Street to Candy Land. I wanted her to buy me one of those large Italian Easter eggs molded from white sugar and elaborately trimmed with pastel ribbons and rosebuds of icing on the outside. Earlier in the week I had examined one closely, and she'd promised me I could have it for an Easter gift. But it wasn't in the Easter basket she'd given me that morning. I was disappointed because I loved holding the viewing end of the egg up to my eye and peeping into the glowing sugar cave, which was nimbly arranged with tiny painted furniture like the room in *Goodnight Moon*, with the kittens and mittens and bowl of mush.

My mother wasn't the scolding type, but once she lurched forward and caught me from behind she didn't let go. Her lips pursed, and then in a strained whisper she said, "We'll talk about the bear later, honey."

"But it wasn't a bear," I said. *"Remember!"*

"How could I forget?" she replied, and held a finger across her lips. "Let's just go home for a while and settle down."

"Can I get the egg first?" I pleaded. I was desperate to get it, desperate to have something to distract me from the image of Mrs. Rumbaugh, who was still pacing room after room in my mind while calling for me to *love, honor, obey,* and *listen to her forever.*

"It's Easter," Mom said softly. "Candy Land is closed. But you will get one. Trust me."

My first impulse was always to trust her rather than fight her, and as I let my disappointment fade I held her hand and kept abreast, my three steps to her two and my two breaths to her three.

We crossed back over Main Street to the Kelly Hotel. The

elevator was broken, and by the time we hiked up the stairs to our third-floor rooms, we were hot.

"Let's just take off our dress clothes for a bit and cool down before going to lunch," she said. It seemed to me that before I could answer she was stripped down near naked. And the moment I saw her a strange door opened within my heart. I was gripped with a sudden fear. It was when I stared at her smooth body that I fully realized she was going to die—not *someday*—but in my lifetime. I stared up at her, and inside I felt a horror that I knew was not just a passing fright. This was a feeling that emerged from deep within me and not from without. I felt limp. The grief of her death was already circulating triumphantly through me as I stood dead still. She had no idea what fear had just captured my heart, and she smiled at me as she lifted her knee and bent forward to deftly roll her stocking down her calf and into a perfect silk doughnut. Her warmth, her pink flesh, her easy way of undressing and hanging up her good clothes with care made her seem so vulnerable. My eternal love for her, by contrast, made her physical life seem temporary and defenseless to me. I was entranced with everything about her—her coal black hair, her woolly smell, her joyful voice that wrapped me in a cocoon of love. She was going to die, and the person I loved heart and soul above all others would be gone and I would be left alone and made tiny and fragile inside the skin of my loneliness and sorrow. I reached out and threw myself against her and pressed my face into her soft belly and the tears poured from my eyes and spilled down her legs like loose pearls. *I will love you and honor you and obey you,* I thought, *and keep you alive in my heart and I will never abandon you at the time of your need. Never.*

She thought the sight of Mrs. Rumbaugh in the basement had overwhelmed me, but it wasn't that at all.

"You'll be fine, pumpkin," she said soothingly, her face lined with concern. "Don't you worry about what those silly old men do." And she stroked my head and wiped the tears with her quick fingers.

Yes, it had been surprising to discover Mrs. Rumbaugh stuffed like a hibernating bear, and although she was spooky, she only really terrified me because she reminded me of my mother's mortality, and in some penetrating way I must have been marked with the knowledge that Ab and Dolph loved their mother as much as I loved mine and that they were driven to preserve her in whatever form they could. In an unspoken way I accepted what they did, and why, and it seemed right—for them and for me. I looked up at my mother and said, "Don't worry. Someday I'll do the same to you, too."

She blanched, and before she realized she had said it she uttered, "Oh, my God, you have the love curse of the—" Then she held her hand over her mouth and stepped away, but it was too late. I had heard her, and somehow I knew I was cursed with loving my mother too much.

"What curse?" I asked innocently.

"You won't understand right now," she said hastily. And to wall off any chance for an explanation, she announced, "Let's get dressed again and go down for Easter lunch." Then tenderly she leaned forward and whispered, "And then to get that egg."

I kissed her on the lips, and my whole mood changed. My troubles dimmed and I felt renewed, as if nothing had happened. The curse had withdrawn in the face of her perfect love. We were making plans together, slipping on our clothes, glancing at our twin selves in the mirror, laughing and fussing with each other like nesting sparrows. And for a time our plans for the present blotted out any worry over an empty future.

We started down the flight of stairs to the first-floor restaurant. Mom was wearing heels and was concentrating on each step as if inching across thin ice. It occurred to me as we slowly descended that behind every closed door in the hotel was a secret. Not as big perhaps as Mrs. Rumbaugh being stuffed and hidden away, but I had an awakening sense that doors were locked not just to keep unwanted people out but to keep secrets captive within.

In an instant this one thought doubled the size of my world, and I suspected the secret side was the more fascinating half. It seemed to me that I was walking inside a maze of secrets. As I drifted down the dimly lit hallway and past the nicked-up doors, each muffled sound, television set, cough, and creaking footfall suggested a blueprint of private worlds that dared me to investigate them. I could feel my skin crawl with the delight and good luck of living in the Kelly Hotel, and it seemed to me the secrets here were as rich and mysterious as any inside an Egyptian pyramid.

Just before we reached the dining room door, I was struck with a question. "What would happen if there were no secrets?" I asked.

"Don't worry," my mother said briskly. "Until you go to heaven, there will always be secrets."

"How do you know?" I asked.

Mom paused. "If nobody had anything to hide, it would mean that everything is allowed," she replied.

"What does that mean?"

"It means if there were no laws," she explained, "people would behave like animals. It would be the survival of the fittest."

That seemed alarming to me. "But nobody really knows what animals are thinking," I said. I was small, and I still liked rules. They made me as large as anyone. But without rules I was just a child. Anyone could do anything they wanted with me.

She bent close toward my face, knowing what I was getting at. "Ab and Dolph are very good people," she said. "You have to realize that. I know it is difficult to believe, but you can't judge them just on what you saw. You have to understand why they did it, and maybe then it will make sense to you. As they say in court: *Audi alteram partem*—'Hear the other side.' "

"I'd love to," I said, wondering what they might say about why they had preserved their mother as if she were one of the kittens they had stuffed and dressed as a Red Cross nurse with a pink-and-white-striped dress and starched white hat.

"I know they are good," I replied. "They love their mother, and nothing can be greater than that."

"You keep believing that rule," she said, smiling broadly, but her lips were just bluffing for her eyes, which narrowed as she studied my face, perhaps for further signs of what she had called "the curse."

In the Kelly Hotel there were two public rooms, which just about everyone in town referred to as "Heaven" and "Hell." There was the tavern on the ground floor and a ladylike dining room directly above it on the first. They were opposites in every way. The tavern was not a room where women who were out shopping would stop for a refreshment or lunch. They had their own location, in the white wicker dining room that Mrs. Kelly had softened with lace sheers over the windows and hooked rugs with summer garden themes of sweet peas and spring onions and zebra tomatoes on the waxed wood floor. The room was heavily scented with tiny watering cans of cinnamon potpourri decorating each round table.

Beneath the dining room, the tavern contributed another sweet smell, like unpicked fruit that had gone to rot. The odor was the combination of southern pine sawdust shoveled thickly across the tavern planks, spilt beer, and tobacco juice. Mr. Kelly always dressed head to toe in starched white bar clothes. He looked like an overcooked ham in sterile bandages and preferred to serve men. Men with girlfriends made him uncomfortable, and married men with girlfriends made him short-tempered. Men who brought their wives in to drink were treated politely but privately scorned as men who "compromised" their wives' reputations. Mr. Kelly never served children in front of the bar but would allow us to order drinks from the kitchen pass-through so we could run them up to guests for tips. But that wasn't often, because the hotel wasn't much of a hotel but more of an apartment building filled with every indigent Kelly in town.

They all—parents, children, aunts, uncles, cousins, nieces, nephews, and grandchildren—lived there and occupied nearly all the rooms, except for the three my mother and I kept and the two briny-smelling rooms that were set aside for men who had to sleep off their beer. The doors to these rooms were kept open for airing out unless they were occupied.

When we entered the dining room Mom stiffened, and her feet stuttered nervously like the hooves of a spooked horse. A group of brightly dressed church ladies had taken over most of the room and were giving a baby shower for a young, very pregnant woman. Her crimson legs were venomously swollen, and she sat with them propped up on an upturned case of Huggies. On the floor below her legs was a damp bar towel and a bowl of ice.

"All the tables are full up," Mrs. Ushock said directly to my mother, and propped her hands on her wide hips, which made her twice as large. Her sharp red elbows stuck out like angry arrowheads. She was a farmer's wife and mother of the young woman. I had often seen her in the pharmacy.

I looked beyond where the ladies had stacked both Easter

gifts and baby gifts on the tables. The back of the room was entirely filled with families out for Easter dinner.

Mom didn't respond to her. "Let's leave," she said quietly to me, and turned to go. I hesitated. Those bloated legs seized me. I couldn't take my eyes off them. The young mother's baby was yet unborn, but already the mother seemed full of decay. Each day the baby would grow stronger, taller, smarter, while the mother became older, weaker, and needier. The fear of my mother's mortality struck me hard again, but before I could dwell on it her strong hand clamped down on the top of my head and she briskly swiveled me around like a potato she was peeling.

"Why can't we wait for a table?" I asked.

"I really don't want to," she said hastily.

"Why?"

"Because Mrs. Ushock and I know a little too much about each other," she said.

"Wouldn't that make you friends?" I asked.

"Or not," she said, hewing her words. "There is such a thing as knowing someone *too* well."

"What do you mean?" I asked. "What do you know about her?"

"It's the other way around," she replied. "But I'll tell you when the time is right."

"Is it a deep secret?" I asked, fishing for any hints of her past, or mine.

"Oh, yes," she said gravely.

"Worse than the stuffed mom?"

"That's hard to top," she whispered. "But this one is pretty good as well."

I knew she had to be referring to my father—a subject for which I showed no curiosity. For a long time I had thought my mother had me by Immaculate Conception. I imagined she simply wanted me so badly that I just appeared—that she prayed for me and nine months later I arrived—an answer to her prayers. It was an answer that was entirely fulfilling because it meant my love for her was as vast as her desire for me.

Who my father was should have been an important question on my mind. But it wasn't. And it wasn't because I was angry about not having a father or was heartbroken. I simply had no interest in one because I had all the love I desired: the right kind of love—mother love. And from the moment I was born I think my mother and I both knew we no longer needed men because, between us, we had all we wished for.

One day I told Sister Nancy that my mother had me just as Mary had Jesus.

Sister smiled. "All life is a miracle," she said. "But you have a father somewhere. Only the Blessed Mother conceived through Immaculate Conception."

I refused to believe her.

After school Sister must have called my mother, because at dinner that night Mom asked if I wanted to know about where I came from. We were eating tomato sandwiches with bacon she had fried up in an electric skillet. She was carefully separating a strip of fat from the lean. I was gazing out the window. Sometimes we didn't look each other in the eye when we spoke because doing so made the room feel too small. I think our time spent staring out at the sky developed our interest in odd weather.

"You know," she reasoned, "I'm going to have to tell you about him someday."

"I don't want to know," I replied matter-of-factly.

"I thought you would say that," she said. "So I've come up with a plan. Whether you want to know or not, I'll tell you when you turn sixteen."

"You don't have to," I said.

"I must," she insisted, and reached out and took my hand. Her touch was an irresistible force, and I could feel myself bending toward her.

"Because of your age," she continued, "I won't tell all the details right now. But trust me, at the moment of your sixteenth birthday I'll tell you every bit of what I know."

"Do you mean there are parts that you don't know?" I asked, thinking that was curious.

"Yes," she answered, and smiled in a way that suggested the mystery was amusing and not frightening. "So maybe you can help me clear up a few things."

That invitation was very satisfying, and I thought, *Okay, I'll wait and then we'll work on it together. It will be a mother-daughter project.*

As Mom had said, I'd find out about my past when the time was right. That suited me fine as we stood in the doorway of the restaurant with Mrs. Ushock looking so hawkish, because suddenly I was no longer interested in an Easter lunch or family secrets but far more interested in the candy egg. I hopped loudly down the steps to the ground floor.

Mrs. Kelly was in the lobby wringing out the steaming head of a filthy mop. Her hands were twisted into knots, and the gray water streamed into a metal bucket. She had bulky upper arms and a large chest, kind of a uni-breast that was tucked under her dress like a bag of laundry. "No rest for the wicked," she grunted, then laughed as she ran a blotchy hand through her damp hair. "If only you could imagine the necks I think of when I choke off this old mop."

Mom jerked her head toward the upstairs restaurant. "I could add a few names to your list," she said.

Mrs. Kelly snorted out loud. "Spare me!" she said, and waved off Mom's thought. "Don't let your past spoil your future."

"True," Mom agreed, and stood a bit taller.

They spoke in adult code, which in my mind looked like a crossword puzzle I couldn't work out.

Mrs. Kelly looked down at me. "Happy Easter, Ivy darling," she said. "I have a little something for you." She gave me a stage wink, which was as bright as a camera flash. She set down her mop and wiped her hands on her dress as she slipped behind the check-in counter. From a lower shelf she lifted out a little basket with the candy egg nestled in shredded pink and green cellophane.

"For you," she said warmly, and swung it toward me. "Happy Easter."

I removed the egg as if it were a newborn baby and peered into the dazzling cave. I examined each object: the little yellow table, the matching chair, the rabbit silhouette on the wall, the tiny basket of colored eggs. Every detail of the interior created an immaculate, radiant world which was perfectly arranged in every way. Each decoration was so spotless and tidy that only pure thoughts and deeds could inhabit the inside. As my mother said, only heaven was a place without secrets, and staring into the egg was like peeking into heaven through a keyhole.

Then I saw the tiny braided rug on the floor, and it reminded me of the little painted rug on which Mrs. Rumbaugh was mounted. Suddenly the egg's perfection was spoiled with the reminder of the bear story the Twins had told me, and that was what put me off more than the stuffed mother. They had lied, like Judas lied to Jesus, and that made me angry.

"It's the same rug," I blurted out to my mom as she turned from Mrs. Kelly. "The rug under the Twins' mom is exactly the same as the one in the egg."

I handed her the egg as if it had turned rotten in my hands. She held the back porthole of the egg toward the overhead light and peeked in. After a moment she lowered it. She smiled and shook her head back and forth with amused astonishment.

"They are so bizarre," she declared lightly, and laughed a bit.

"They're creepy," I whispered.

Mom looked up toward Mrs. Kelly, who seemed to be paying too much attention, and before I could say more about what I had seen in the basement she instructed me to use my manners.

"Thank you, Mrs. Kelly," I said, smiling with the egg held tightly between my two hands.

"You're welcome, darling," she replied, stepping out from behind the counter to give me a kiss.

Then Mom and I walked back up the stairs, quickly past the restaurant, and past the hallway of secrets, which reminded me that Mrs. Kelly and Mom were speaking in code.

"Why does everyone know more about me than me?" I asked.

"Ivy," Mom said, "you are the lucky one. You get to live in a world full of secrets while all of theirs have been answered."

That stumped me for a moment. "But that's not fair!" I cried out. "I want answers, too."

"When you are sixteen," she said playfully. "Unless you want to know now?"

I covered my ears with my hands. "I don't want to hear any more," I sang. "Sorry I asked!" The thought of knowing anything about my father threatened my all-consuming love for my mother.

By the time we entered our rooms my mind had seized on another idea.

"I was wondering," I asked. "Do the Twins play with their mother as if she were a big doll? I mean if they just have her hidden around the house like a Halloween decoration, it's pretty scary. But it doesn't seem frightening to me at all if when they play they say 'Yes, Mother' and 'No, Mother' and are being really sweet as they wheel her around the pharmacy displays and help her shop. And I wonder what kind of voice they make to imitate her. Would it be a high-pitched voice like a parrot squawking, 'Abner, you eat your vegetables' and 'Adolph, you get back to work!' Or would it be some old man's froggy voice trying to squeak out a lady's voice?"

"I couldn't begin to tell you," Mom replied. "I've never heard them talk for her. You have to remember they don't want anyone knowing about her. It's a *secret.*"

"Why?" I asked.

"It's against the law," Mom said dramatically. "Which is why you can't mention this to anyone or they might be put in jail."

"Okay," I said. It seemed easy enough to forgive them. Even though they had lied to me, I could understand why because Mom had said they could be sent to jail.

At the time I didn't realize their lie was a defense against the fear they had of losing their mother. I was still too young to understand that most lies were not about stealing or fighting or cheating but were just ways by which a person shrinks their whole world down to a size they can keep protected in the palm of one hand.

"Look!" She pointed toward the pharmacy.

Across the street the Twins were peeking out at us from their upstairs windows. As soon as Mom pointed at them, they closed the blinds.

"Don't be afraid of the Twins," she advised. "They're like two befuddled kids, and in a way I think it's up to us to take care of them. Well, at least I thought I always had to."

I smiled to myself. It was just as I thought. I scared them more than they scared me. It was a certain kind of power I felt over them. Instead of being reduced by what they thought of me, I now felt larger with the thoughts I had about them. I liked that.

IT RUNS IN THE FAMILY

Ever since kindergarten I had spent my after-school hours waiting at the pharmacy until Mom's bus delivered her from work. I loved the pharmacy with its marble ice cream counter and my basement cottage and even the two brothers while they squabbled and disagreed and corrected each other as they wildly slashed up the aisles and past the counters like two pole-crossed magnets stubbornly resisting each other in their halfhearted struggle to remain distinct. The pharmacy marked the center of town, and when people came in to shop and talk I greeted them and helped guide them to products on the shelves. To keep me occupied the Twins would give me little jobs like writing prices on bottles of aspirin with a black marker and sorting out the toothbrush choices by bristle strength and handing out sample-size bottles of hand lotion and dandruff shampoo. There were many times when I said to Ab and Dolph, "I want to be a pharmacist like you." But this only seemed to make them nervous.

"You do as your mother says," Ab would remind me.

"She'll always know what's best," Dolph would add.

She did. Mom and Sister Nancy planned for me to enter a life of religious service. And after what I had seen in the basement, I was happy with their plan. A calling into the church seemed better to me than a *calling* from Mrs. Rumbaugh.

Seeing the Twins' mother like that was pretty shocking. I couldn't entirely put the discovery of her out of my mind. I tried to think of other things. Wholesome thoughts. But there were compelling feelings deep down in my gut that were stronger than my effort to resist. I simply could not stop dwelling on the image of that preserved mother. I thought something was wrong with me. Why couldn't I put her out of my mind? Why was I attracted to what was perverse? And why was I compelled to know more?

My mother knew, but she was waiting to tell me until—as she said—"you are mature enough to control your future."

So on the Monday morning after Easter, while we were getting dressed, she said, "I've come up with a different after-school arrangement. From now on you'll return to the hotel and Mrs. Kelly will watch over you."

I was happy to do what she said. When it came to fulfilling her orders, obedience and contentment always felt the same to me.

Just then Mrs. Kelly knocked on our door. When I opened it, she gave me a dog-friendly pat on my head hard enough to buckle my knees.

"Good morning, Ivy," Mrs. Kelly said brightly. "Your Mom

and I spoke last night after you conked out and we decided that I'm the lucky one who gets to watch over you."

I nodded. "Mom was just telling me," I said.

"Now, don't be afraid to ask me to help with anything if you need me," she added. "Remember, you are an honorary Kelly. Okay?" She reached out and again patted me on the head until I stepped back. "And you're probably a lot easier to care for than most of these luckless shamrocks." She laughed at her own remark and afterward had to lean forward and adjust her chest from having jostled it out of place.

"Yes, thank you," I said, and kissed her on the cheek.

She kissed me back, then marched down the hall with some pressing chore in mind. She was a heavy walker, and after she was out of sight I could still feel her solid footfalls humming through the floorboards. There was something happy in that vibration, like a song that makes you feel good when you sing it.

Just then my mother caught me from behind and gave me a big hug. I knew she was pleased with me, and there was nothing I loved more than to make her love me even more. At times like this, when she hugged me so tightly, I thought I'd rather be recessed inside her than be my own person, as if being her heart and pumping blood through her veins all day and night from the red niche of her chest would be more satisfying than looking into the mirror and seeing my own living face.

"Now, don't you think we are off to a good start?" Mom asked, releasing me and right away fussing with my hair.

"Oh, yes," I said, holding still. "I like Mrs. Kelly."

"And I trust her," Mom added, adjusting a barrette. "I'm glad we've worked this out so smoothly."

It was easy for her to feel confident that everything would be fine leaving me at the hotel. First, I wasn't the kind of girl who would run off without telling someone where I was going. And Mount Pleasant was the kind of small town where I knew most people by sight and they knew me.

After school that day I walked back to the hotel and checked in with Mrs. Kelly, who was downstairs at the front desk talking on the phone.

"I'm home, Mrs. Kelly," I announced, and waved to her.

"Hi, sugar," she whispered, covering the mouthpiece for a moment. "Go on up to your room."

The elevator was still broken, and I lugged my backpack up the stairs as her voice followed, gleefully ordering another ten pounds of rose petal potpourri, as if she were ordering a bucket of rubies. After I unlocked the door and entered our drowsy rooms the first thing I did was glance up at the clock. Mom would be home in two and a half hours. I knew I had to stay busy otherwise the clock would move slowly. I cleaned up our little corner kitchenette. I washed the breakfast dishes and hand-mopped the dirty tan linoleum floor. I made the double bed we shared. I tidied up the bathroom and then sat down to do my math homework. After that I made a birthday card for a schoolmate. We were doing a class play with Egyptian costumes, so next I practiced walking back and forth across the room as if I were flat with one crooked arm held up in front of me like a bent snake and the other hooked down behind me like a crimped tail.

When I tired of that, I opened my mother's closet and put on her clothes—not her good ones but the too-tight ones we shared because they were a little too young-looking on her and a little too old-looking on me. They made us more like sisters.

And then I waited. I sat on the ottoman and looked out our third-floor window and down at the pharmacy and surrounding streets. I had spent many hours of my life looking out that window, and nothing much ever changed. The pharmacy was a three-story brick-and-red-stone building. The Twins had designed it as if it was a gothic temple to medicine, and they were very proud of their work. Along the roof were lined a half-dozen spires with carved ferns running up their sides, and on top of each spire was a white stone apothecary jar. Just below the edge of the roof were four round oculus windows, which looked like pirate cannon ports aiming directly at the Kelly Hotel. At times it seemed they were about to let loose a broadside and blow us to smithereens. At other times the beams of sunlight reflected off those windows and shined into our rooms like spotlights. We stood within them and dramatically delivered fake lines as if we were theater stars onstage.

The middle floor of the building had two deep and dark interior porches with heavy parapets of rubbed red stone, from which the Twins hung flags on national holidays or black swag when anyone from the church died. The burglar who had broken into the drug room had jumped out over the top of the parapet after the Twins heard him and blocked his exit on the ground floor. He broke his leg upon impact and was captured up the street huddled in the orange doorway of the boarded-up Rexall.

Though the Twins had been robbed, they tracked down the burglar, set his leg, and gave him enough medication to satisfy his drug dependency until an ambulance arrived and he could be taken to a hospital. They never pressed charges, explaining to my mother that the broken leg was "God's punishment enough." My mother disagreed. She worked in the criminal court and knew a broken leg was no deterrent to a drug addiction.

But the united force of the Twins' minds was immovable. They would not charge him.

"Suit yourself," my mother said curtly. "You can be both *judge* and *jury*, but I guarantee you he'll be back. Don't get me wrong, I'd love to see him rehabilitated, but once people are inflicted with a craving it never goes away. You might control it, but you will never fully stop it."

Once she put it that way, I understood the burglar's plight. I was not addicted to drugs, but I was addicted to my mother and there was no cure and even if there was I wouldn't want it anyway. Mine was an affliction I did not resent. After all, who could resent love?

Below the pharmacy balcony along Main Street were two tall picture windows. Between the windows stood a thin column that was finished with a keystone capital from which supporting ribs, like black eyebrows, arched across the full sheets of thick glass.

The windows allowed shoppers to look directly into the store, and allowed Ab and Dolph to look directly back like two nearsighted hoot owls with their fixed pupils and rotating necks. They never blocked the view with hanging advertisements or bright product displays. They never had a sale. Whenever they had products that they no longer wanted, or had expired, they gave them to the church. "That's what a tithe is," Ab explained to me when he was thinning the inventory. "Ten percent of what we make goes to the ten percent that can't."

"What's that mean?" I asked.

"It means that ten percent of the population is either disabled or feebleminded," he said matter-of-factly. "Mother Nature isn't perfect, so it's man's duty to help those who can't help themselves."

When he said that I wondered why it was that some people were less than perfect. It seemed that nature also had secrets locked behind closed doors. What was nature hiding? It was puzzling that we were not all one and the same when at school I was constantly taught that in the eyes of church and state we were all created equal.

"Don't fret," he said, reading the confused look on my face. "Science will figure it out. Someday there'll be procedures to make up for nature's faults. You'll receive a gene implant and not be mentally diminished or diseased, but until then it's up to us to shoulder the burden."

Won't that be wonderful? I thought. Someday science would make us all truly equal so nature's faults could no longer leave some people with less, because I wanted Mother Nature to be as perfect as my own mother.

So that first day under Mrs. Kelly's care I waited patiently at the window and stared over at the pharmacy building. Each time a bus arrived I perked up like a puppy waiting for its owner, then slumped back down when it wasn't Mom's. I had memorized what she wore to work, and when the five-thirty pulled in, I saw just a snatch of her favorite plaid jacket through the window and my heart began to pound. Then I saw her black patent-leather heel emerge from the bus and step toward the curb, and by that time I was waving wildly. She knew to look up at the window and smile and wave back. She stepped forward to allow the others off behind her, and as she walked toward me she blew me kiss after kiss until the air was filled with them like soap bubbles whooshing this way and that up and up to the window until they popped against my lips and cheeks and eyes and my face was like the bright center of a sunflower surrounded by the gentle petals of her kisses.

Once she disappeared from sight, I hopped up and dashed down the stairs to greet her in the lobby. She knelt as I ran into her arms.

"How's my brave girl?" she asked, giving me a good look.

"Brave," I replied, squinting with savage bravery. I didn't want her to worry, and so I lied as best I could.

On the following day my morning started out well. Early recess went smoothly. From when I was in kindergarten I played a game by myself where I'd imagine what my mother would be doing, and I would do it, too, as if there were invisible but strong wires attached to our joints, like long-distance puppet strings. I would stand out at recess behind the soot-black Polish church with my eyes closed and arms held out and hands poised as if typing, just as she did, and I would cock my head to one side and bite down on my lower lip, as she did, and with my fingers would tap-tap-tap away at the air while hers were furiously recording at the steno machine in the Greensburg courtroom. Sometimes I'd play like I was taking a break. I'd walk the coal ash playground as if following a hallway, stand in line at the snack bar and wait my turn, buy a Coke, go a few more steps, and open a small door that led up a cramped flight of stairs to the top of the courthouse dome, where I would sip my Coke and look up at the sky and watch for unusual weather patterns like counterclockwise circulations and wind-shear formations and I'd make little notes on a pad about "seasonal affective disorder" and weather-influenced crime rates. Afterward I'd reapply my lipstick and return down the cramped stairs and reenter the judge's office to report on my atmospheric theories. "Humidity is rising," I would announce gravely. "Crime will increase."

These are things my mother told me she did during the day, and so I did them, too. This all seemed so innocent at first—just a young girl growing up to become exactly like her mother. What could be more natural?

Then at lunch recess something happened. At first I was running wildly with a pack of girls across the playground and screaming at the top of my lungs, and this distracted me from all thoughts of my mother. But that was a temporary relief. Suddenly the color of a spring leaf on an elm tree reminded me of the leaf appliqué on the sweater set she was wearing that day, and instantly the dread of her looming death sent me into a spiral of fear. I panicked. I didn't know what was happening. My heart raced.

The fear was very potent; still I tried to fight back. I imagined kissing my mother's hands and neck like a pet. I pictured myself brushing her hair and painting her nails, bringing her a cup of tea, and preparing her bath. But these made-up happy scenes did not save me from my fear. I needed the real her. I fled the playground while ignoring the teacher's calls to come back.

I ran the five blocks to the hotel. The lobby was empty, and I stamped up the stairs and pounded on our door.

"Mom! Mom!" I shouted. "Please let me in. Please!" I just knew Mom had come home sick or hurt and needed me, and I was blind to the truth that it was I who needed her.

I had left my door key taped inside my lunch box at school. I raced down to the lobby and took the passkey from behind the counter and ran back up. I opened the door and scrambled through the rooms calling out for her. Of course she was at work.

The school called Mrs. Kelly, who came into the room and found me curled up under the covers on Mom's side of the bed, my head slipped into the exact pillow dimple where hers had rested. The darkness and the faint scent of Mom's skin on the sheets had calmed me. Mrs. Kelly sat on the edge of the bed and patted my hand.

"There, there," she cooed. "You're fine. Your mother's fine."

She tried to soothe my fears, but I didn't listen to her words, yet her voice was a fountain of comforting sounds.

When Mom returned home I hopped up and was suddenly purring like a cat overflowing with contentment. By then she had had a talk with Sister Nancy and, after a few words with Mrs. Kelly, wanted to talk with me. I told her my fears about her dying. She assured me how safe she was in court, and how young and healthy she was. It meant nothing. I knew the moment she was out of sight she was doomed and it would always be up to me to keep her safe, and to keep her by my side.

"Why do you think you feel this way?" she asked, petting my hair.

"You already told me," I said, looking up into her face. "I've got a love curse."

"Honey," she said tenderly, "I was wrong. It is not a curse to love me."

"I know," I said. "Loving you is what I live for. It is the fear of losing you that is the curse."

"You mustn't worry," she said, kissing me. "You will never lose me."

That simple line, *you will never lose me*, somehow changed my whole mood, and I began to pull out of the state I was in. *I will never lose her*, I thought, *because it is not up to her to leave me but up to me to keep her*—and I planned to always keep her by my side.

That night we sat in front of the TV, both of us knitting, and the sound of the needles clicking as the knots came together was an enormous comfort. "Maybe you can just knit after school and make an afghan for the couch?"

"It's no fun to do it alone," I said, and made a long face.

"Then maybe you need a hobby," she suggested. "Some fresh new activity to keep you busy."

That appealed to me. "Yes," I said. "I'll give it a chance."

The next day after school I checked in with Mrs. Kelly, who now looked at me more carefully, as if I had been something beautiful, like a fancy vase, that had been dropped. She scanned me up and down and around, as if searching for the cracks where I had been glued back together.

"I'm going to go down to the library," I said to her. "I need to find a book on hobbies."

"An excellent idea," she replied a bit too brightly. "When I was a girl I cut out magazine pictures of fancy hats and shoes and pasted them in a scrapbook. It kept me occupied for hours."

"I think I need to do something with my hands," I said, holding them in front of me as if they were two tiny, embryonic people. "They need some training," I explained while wiggling the fingers.

"Have fun," she said, then went back to sewing green *K*'s onto new bath towels.

The library was on Main Street, and I walked there in minutes. Once inside I asked the librarian, Mr. Fenton, for books on hobbies. "Not just kid hobbies," I explained. "Or girl hobbies, but all kinds of hobbies."

He stood and with long, deliberate strides lunged forward as if he had a limit on the number of steps he was allotted each day. He pointed out the shelf of hobby books, then just as deftly returned to his desk.

It didn't take long to know what I was there for. Once I saw the book on taxidermy, it seemed so obvious. I pulled it from the shelf and flipped through the pages—*Taxidermy for Fun and Profit*. The sensation was riveting. I can only say that it must have been something like when Joan of Arc spoke to the archangel Michael in her garden. I had a vision of my mother not in heaven but here on earth. She was sitting in a chair holding a book in her hands reading out loud. She was dead, but her lips were moving and her recorded voice was coming from a little speaker embedded in her chest. Some people might call this the hallucination of an unfit mind. But it wasn't that to me. It was a vision as clear and purposeful and embracing as any romantically maternal moment I've ever felt. *Of course*, I thought, *I will need to record her voice, too*.

I marched to the front desk and immediately checked out the book.

When I left the library, I went down to the hobby shop and bought some supplies. With my Easter money I bought plaster of paris, and thick wire, and wooden dowels. I couldn't afford the special tools illustrated in the taxidermy guidebook, but Mom had some hand tools at home she kept in an old cigar box. I could use them, I figured. The book listed special chemicals, too, but the hobby shop didn't carry them. *I'll figure that out later*, I thought.

I returned to the hotel and hid everything I had bought, plus the book, in the dresser drawer of one of the empty hotel rooms. Then I dashed upstairs, and just before the five-thirty bus stopped in front of the pharmacy I was sitting at the window. When she stepped off and looked toward me I was waving wildly, my heart full of love and joy. Then I ran downstairs to greet her at the door.

"How'd it go today?" she asked, her voice as upbeat as birdsong.

"Much better," I said, nodding happily. "I think a hobby is the answer."

"Find anything you might like?"

"I'm working on it," I replied coyly, smiling secretly to myself. I wanted to surprise her.

That night I was calm, and the next day at school I was, too. It was as if I had stopped fighting something. I wasn't sure if I had defeated an enemy within me or had been captured without resistance. But I was at peace.

The following day I put my new hobby to work. I gathered some stuffed animals and a large rag doll and tools from upstairs and went down to the hotel room and locked the door. I carried everything into the bathroom and set out all my equipment as if I were in an operating room. I had the tools and hobby supplies on the counter. In the sink I had the plaster of paris. I dropped my stuffed animals into the dry bathtub. I opened my taxidermy book and read a few pages, then got busy. I took the rag doll and cut open the length of her belly. I pulled out the old shredded cloth stuffing and handful by handful threw it into the toilet. I didn't want to clog it up, so I flushed often. When I had completely removed the stuffing, I took the wire and began to build an armature inside the cloth skin as if I were filling her full of bones. I ran short of wire, but luckily there were wire coat hangers in the closet and they twisted up just fine. Once I had the body stretched out on the armature, I mixed the plaster of paris and with a spoon began to work it down into her limbs as the book had advised. From the moisture leaking through the cloth the skin became blotchy, but I figured I could blow-dry it later, then paint it.

When I had stuffed it full, I began to sew the belly back up. While I worked the stitches as finely as I could, I drifted into thinking more about preserving Mother. She would get bored in the same outfits, so I'd collect an entire wardrobe and dress and undress her for all specific occasions, from cocktail gowns to church clothes to business suits. I'd get her wigs too, just like my dolls had. It would also be helpful for her to have bendable joints so she could sit down with me for dinner. And if I could disconnect her limbs and fold her up into a suitcase,

I could take her on trips. Around the house I could have her on wheels with a little electric motor and steer her from room to room like those remote-control cars. I was entirely cheerful with these thoughts while I completed the sewing.

Before the plaster set too firmly, I twisted the legs so that the doll could sit on the counter, and I put her arms on her hips and cocked her head to one side. She looked a little sassy. I glanced out at the bedside clock. It was almost time for my mother to come home, so I turned off the bathroom light, pulled the door closed, and ran upstairs.

When Mom got off the bus I was waiting at the window, and as before I ran down to greet her. She didn't ask how my day had been because she could tell I was so carefree. We walked to the grocery store. "We'll have opposite day," she announced. "Eggs and bacon for dinner."

I always loved opposite day. "Can we sleep upside down in bed, too?" I asked. We had done that before. And we walked backward through the rooms and pronounced our names backward and said just the opposite of what we meant.

"Not tonight," she said, slumping a bit. "It's all I can do to think forward, but we'll do it soon."

That was fine with me. I was in such a good mood nothing could upset me. We walked home, and she cooked at the stove and I made cinnamon toast and she talked about her day and the medical malpractice suit she was recording. A woman was diagnosed with twins, but when she gave birth there was only one baby. She was suing her pediatrician for incorrect medical information and for trauma because she had already "bonded" with the second child.

"What happened to the other baby?" I asked.

"I shouldn't tell you this," Mom said, "but it's so bizarre I can't get it out of my mind. The defense called in a doctor who testified that some twin fetuses seem to swallow the other twin. He cited a medical case where an autopsy was performed on a grown man who had died, and when he was cut open they found a complete fetus, like a tumor in him. He had swallowed it when in his mother's belly and somehow it had remained inside him all his life."

This story suddenly began to make me wonder if inside me there was another me that had just recently awakened, like a second little self telling me what to do, taking control, steering me toward my hobby. "Maybe that's what's happening to me," I said.

She gave me a terrified look as if I had just broken out with a pox. "I'm sorry," she said, and bit down on her lip. "I shouldn't have brought this up. It's awful dinner conversation."

"No, it's okay," I said. "I've been thinking about the love curse. Maybe this is what's going on inside me, because I've been different from my usual self."

"No," she said, suddenly rushing around the table and sweeping me into her arms. "Don't start thinking about that again. There is nothing wrong with you."

And then there was a loud knock at the door, which startled both of us.

I never imagined anyone would rent a hotel room that night. But they did, and they must have gotten a shock when they went into the bathroom that I had been using as a workshop.

"Hello, June?" Mrs. Kelly called forcefully, and knocked loudly again before Mom could respond.

When Mom opened the door, I heard Mrs. Kelly say in a puzzled voice, "What do you think this is?"

"It must belong to Ivy," Mom said. "But it looks kind of odd."

"I'm beginning to think she needs some extra help," Mrs. Kelly said in a hushed voice. "Take a good look at what she's done here. This isn't right. Even my boys weren't like this, and they were half-cracked."

"I'll speak to her," Mom replied. By then I had slipped around beside her and looked up at Mrs. Kelly.

She was holding the rag doll in her hand. It was lumpy and misshapen. Maybe the hotel guest had thrown it across the room. It was still damp, and lines of plaster had leaked out where I had sewn it up. Mrs. Kelly handed it to Mom. "I have to run," she said. "I need to take care of the guest. He's pickled to begin with, and now he's gotten all psychotic-like."

"Offer him a drink on me," Mom said.

"That's the last thing he needs," Mrs. Kelly snapped, her voice already trailing down the hall over the thumps of her footfalls.

As soon as Mom closed the door I dreaded what she might say, so I spoke first. "I know why she said I needed help."

Mom looked at me with a puzzled expression on her face. In her hands was the oddly shaped doll. "Why would Mrs. Kelly say that?" she asked quietly.

"Because I didn't do it right," I said, reaching forward and pulling the doll from her hands. I squeezed its slumping, twisted body, but the plaster wouldn't even out. I gave it a shake. I was so frustrated. "It shouldn't be lumpy. And it should look real. And now it's ruined."

I stomped over to the kitchen and furiously stuffed it into the trash bin.

"I think you need more supervision," my mother said.

"I think so, too," I replied.

"I think we are talking about two different things," she said. "I think you need some healthy activities, and you think you need help with your home taxidermy."

I nodded. "Yes," I said, "I need help. I'm doing it all wrong."

"I can't afford after-school care," Mom said.

"Don't worry," I replied. "I'm going to return to the pharmacy."

"I thought you were angry with them," she reminded me.

"I've gotten over it," I replied. And I had.

2
NINE YEARS LATER

A devil, a born devil, on whose nature
Nurture can never stick.
—William Shakespeare

THE RUMBAUGHS

Everyone complained about the weather. For the farmers the summer was too cool and soggy. Tomatoes didn't ripen. Corn rotted. Melons were watery and bitter. For the miners the coal was damp and tunnels were prone to flood. Construction projects were abandoned. Shoppers stayed at home. Even the birds looked defeated with their soggy nests. The weather forecasters blamed El Niño for the constant rain, but Mom reasoned it was upper tropospheric cold cores causing the weather malaise.

"You know what I love about the weather?" she might say to me after staring out the window for a long spell.

"No," I'd reply. "I really don't."

"I find it so fascinating," she would continue, "that what people can't control seems to utterly control them. The more they fight it the more they fail. For some people if it is not a bright sunny sky they don't see any beauty in the sky at all.

When they don't get what they want, they can't appreciate what they are given. I don't trust anyone who wants to control the weather. People want too much power over nature. Don't you think so?"

I had no argument with nature. Since the time when I was seven years old and the love curse for my mother unfolded inside me, I seemed to be living a life driven by a genetic engine from within. I allowed the curse to guide me in my thoughts and deeds, and as a result I was not conflicted with doubt and uncertainty, as were so many people my age who struggled to become something they were not—struggled to imitate something outside themselves, instead of discovering who they already were.

And then I turned sixteen.

It was a Saturday. The weather cleared for a short spell, and after I had opened some presents my mother and I decided to take a drive through the countryside. She borrowed Ab and Dolph's rusting Mercedes, and we set out with a picnic lunch and high hopes as the sun shined down on us.

We had been in the car only a few minutes when she said, "I've held off telling you everything about me and your origins until your sixteenth birthday. I just want you to know that no matter what you think you know, what you have guessed at, or how you feel now, you are in for a big birthday surprise, and when you get it you will not believe it. You will refuse it, but I swear it is the greatest gift I can give you."

I reached across the seat and gently rested my hand on her

smooth shoulder, then quietly took a long, slow breath. Touching her was always so vital to me. There was something bountiful in our physical connection, as if my hand against her body was some sort of umbilical cord passing nourishment between us.

"Don't worry," I said. "I'm ready."

I had been waiting for this day for many years and I was prepared. As I grew up I had thought a lot about the nature of *questions* and *answers*. Those two words seemed as inseparable as Chang and Eng and were like a set of manacles in my mind. I believed that no person, or emotion, or idea was alone unto itself but was understood only against the contrast of its opposite. An action had no purpose without a reaction. Hope was never so courageous as when pitted against cynicism. Love was made more powerful when hate dissolved into it. Perhaps because I had spent so much time with Ab and Dolph, I had an odd suspicion my mother was going to tell me I had a twin, but it turned out to be a twin of another kind. It was just that my questions were finally paired up face-to-face with the answers.

She drove me out to the old Lutheran church in Carpentertown. It was called the Rumbaugh Church because from the time that Hermann Rumbaugh had built it after the Civil War the Rumbaughs had privately funded it, and all of them were buried out back.

"This is where I want to be buried," she said, as we pulled up a narrow driveway toward a modest red-brick building with a white wooden steeple. We came to a stop and rolled up the windows. The recent moisture had settled into the leather seats, and the air smelled of mildew. I mentioned this. Mom sniffed.

"Smells more like an old coffin," she declared. There was an edge to her voice. She mashed down on the emergency brake as if she were going to stop the rotation of the earth. We opened and closed the car doors and as silently as cats walked a thin brick path to the back of the church. The quiet between us was filled with the arbitrary sounds of nature, but there was nothing arbitrary within us.

She had a key borrowed from the Twins, and we entered through the back, walked around to the front of the altar, and continued down the short central aisle until we took a seat in the last oak pew. I set the picnic basket between us.

"When you are from a small town," she said in a church whisper, "you realize that it is the small details in life that add up to something extraordinary. And now that you have turned sixteen, I'll give you all the details and you can add them up for yourself and find where you stand in all of this. But you won't understand a thing about this mother love curse until you understand the Rumbaughs, so I'll start with them."

"Does this have to do with my father?" I asked testily, because I still had no interest in him.

She held up a finger to silence me. "Look," she said. "I've been thinking about this day for many years, and I have mapped out what I want to say, so just bear with me. Okay?"

"Okay," I said, and sat back. From working in the court-house she told me a lot of stories, and it always seemed her effort to tell them had to be matched by my effort to remember them, and to remember them was a way of preserving her within me.

Then she told me what she knew of the Rumbaugh history, and the more I heard the more I understood—not just about who I was but where I was going, and why.

The Rumbaughs arrived in western Pennsylvania from Germany in the early 1800s, she began. Some said the first Rumbaughs came even earlier, as Hessian troops hired by the British during the Revolutionary War and stationed in Trenton, New Jersey. After Washington crossed the Delaware and routed the enemy, a Rumbaugh was reported to have slipped away into the woods, heading west with a native woman twice his age. I doubt there's any proof of that, but knowing what I do about the love curse, I rather doubt a Rumbaugh would have come to the colonies and left his mother behind.

The first Rumbaughs that Mom could trace within the United States were field and feed farmers in the early 1800s, but they soon branched out. By the Civil War one of them, Hermann Rumbaugh, was making a lot of money through charging families who had lost loved ones in battle a fee to return their bodies. It seems many Union soldiers had taken out life insurance policies, and their families could receive the death benefit from the insurance company only upon proof of death. Their bodies were often pieced together from disparate parts stuffed into intact uniforms, but it was the face that was significant for identification. The insurance companies needed to see the body—the face to be exact—as fingerprinting was not yet invented and identity documents were often forged to claim a false death benefit while allowing the soldier to desert.

Embalming, back then, was the new "body preservation science." A company called the Egyptian Chemical Co. sold the necessary fluids, and Hermann used a portable battlefield hand pump to pump the embalming fluid into a main artery, which then forced the remaining blood out an existing wound or a slit he provided in another artery. Then he'd cart or rail-transport the bodies back from the battlefield to be identified, and payment would be sent to his mother, naturally.

"Pardon me for saying so," my mother said sheepishly, "but Hermann made a killing." She told me he had teams of freed slaves working the battlefields for him. Hermann kept lists of all the troops organized into regiments and battle positions so he could narrow down where the insured might have fallen. His men would fan out and sort through the casualties, matching insurance policy photographs to faces. Then they'd find intact, presentable uniforms and fill them with whatever extra body parts were needed to compose a respectable corpse and top it off with the proper head, hat, and rankings.

Hermann provided this body retrieval service throughout the Union. It was a lucrative business, and by the time the Battle of Gettysburg was over he had amassed a small fortune.

Mom said family lore has it he claimed to have gotten into a tug-of-war with the Civil War photographer Mathew Brady over bodies that they both wanted—Brady for his staged post-battle photographs and Hermann for his bounty. I laughed at the thought of this—the pushing and shoving and the blood and bits flying—but it was a nervous laughter.

After Gettysburg the Union Army marched south and the killing continued. Hermann further added to his fortune by expanding his business to include Southern families. While watching Union soldiers bury dead Confederates in mass graves, he examined many of the corpses and found identification. He embalmed and iced them, contacted their families through couriers and newspaper ads, and sold them back for a steep price.

By the time the fighting was over, he was exhausted with death. It was said he wanted only to return to his mother, whom he loved *and* who had managed his money. After the war he built an elaborate Victorian farmhouse for himself, his wife, and his children. On an adjoining piece of property he built a smaller version of the same house for his mother. Beneath the two houses he constructed a tunnel, so he could rush to his mother's side no matter the time of day or weather.

"I don't know how he treated his own wife and kids," Mom said, "but he's not buried next to them, which should tell you something."

In fact, after his mother died, Hermann personally embalmed her and then in grief committed suicide through arsenic poisoning, leaving strict instructions to be embalmed himself and buried with her in a double-wide coffin he had commissioned. His widow followed his instructions, then promptly moved in with one of her sons, Peter, who was a mink farmer.

While my mother told me all of this, it made her so anxious she had to take breaks. She'd stand up and walk over to the front door of the church and open it.

"It's a little stale in here," she said. "Some sun and fresh air will do it good."

She was always in favor of fresh air.

"Yes," I replied, and took a deep breath. What was good for her was good for me. "Do you want something to drink?" I asked. She liked fresh water, too.

She took a deep breath at the door and then returned to the pew. "I better keep talking," she said as I handed her a bottle of water. "Or we'll be here all night."

Peter Rumbaugh—father of Ab and Dolph—was very success- ful at breeding minks for their most in-demand millinery traits: fur length, color, luster, and strength. Peter knew of Mendel's early genetic experiments with crossbreeding peas and used the same selective breeding techniques to breed supe- rior minks. He and his robust wife of Nordic descent had twelve children, the last two of which were the Twins. Peter was very proud of his family—a family that had never suffered a death during childbirth, or from any disease, including the great worldwide influenza epidemic of 1918–19, which ended many lives around here.

In 1921 Mr. Rumbaugh took his entire family to the Westmoreland County Fair. He belonged to the American Animal Breeders Association, and they were sponsoring a new exhibit for the recently founded American Eugenics and Health Society.

The idea of eugenics, my mother explained, was put forward by Sir Francis Galton, who was a cousin to Charles Darwin. In 1865 Galton introduced the theory that all great civilizations could base their success upon superior genes and that all undercivilized cultures had inferior genes. Naturally he concluded that Nordic and Aryan genes were paramount.

The Eugenics Research Association was located in Cold Spring Harbor, Long Island, run by Charles Benedict Davenport, and funded by the Carnegie Foundation for Experimental Evolution. Mr. Rumbaugh, already familiar with commonsense genetics through mink breeding, was immediately drawn to the ERA position that there was a biological basis for the Superior Family. He had read Madison Grant's vastly successful book, *The Passing of the Great Race*, which was serialized in the *Pittsburgh Gazette-Times*, and had memorized passages that he found especially relevant, and he quoted Grant's dictum that "the cross between a white man and a Hindu is a Hindu, and the cross between a white man and a Negro is a Negro; and a cross between any of the three European races and a Jew is a Jew." As far as anyone knew,

Mr. Rumbaugh had never seen a Hindu, a Negro, or a Jew in Mount Pleasant.

The eugenics booth at the county fair sponsored a Fitter Family contest. Each family that applied was charted for tuberculosis, delirium tremens, syphilis, hair color, eye color, skin pigmentation, mental traits, epilepsy, diabetes, and financial status as well as alcoholism, criminal behavior, sexual misconduct, and religious beliefs. The final test was administered by a nurse who used a pair of steel calipers to measure their cranium size, since it was commonly believed that the inferior races had smaller heads and, as a result, smaller brains.

After all the families were interviewed and their "Human Stock" pedigrees charted and craniums scientifically navigated, the Rumbaugh family received the gold medal at the fair for superior genetics. The medal showed a young child reaching up toward his loving parents. Around the outer face of the medal it read, "Yea, I Have a Goodly Heritage"—this of course being the same Fitter Family medal that I had seen every day in the pharmacy. I loved that medal. When no one was looking I used to wear it around my neck as if I'd won the Rumbaugh gold medal at the Olympics.

Mr. Rumbaugh was also delighted with his gold medal and immediately joined the Eugenics Research Association. He was just in time to travel to New York City and attend the Second International Congress of Eugenics. When he returned home, he boasted not only of meeting the highly honored Madison Grant but of traveling to the New York Zoological

Park, where Grant was a founding member and responsible for keeping a genuine African Pygmy locked up on display. Peter bragged that he even fed the Pygmy a banana.

One of the ERA's weaknesses was in the area of scientific proof that Nordic and Aryan genes were superior to all others. They could point to the great European races and their advanced cultures and civilizations, and they could list an honor roll of American and European captains of industry, soldiers, scholars, and presidents, but they could never entirely convince the truly objective scientists, who were more inclined to form opinions on the "nature versus nurture" argument around hard facts rather than racial features and "dummy Darwinism."

The ERA was pretty eager to gather scientific proof that eugenics was an indisputable science which isolated and labeled factors that would predict refined personal habits, greater intelligence, and social respectability. All their charts and graphs of how superior hereditary traits stayed within race lines were dismissed as mere speculation by scientists who looked more toward environmental conditions to mold behavior. This is why the study of twins was chosen as the perfect way to gather proof for the eugenics cause. With twins the ERA would show the world that it was bloodlines and not the environment that made the man. And so Peter entered into a secret agreement with the ERA so they would become legal guardians for the Twins. One morning he sent his wife to Pittsburgh to purchase mink hats for samples, and while she was gone he packed the Twins' trunks, dressed them, kissed them, and instructed them to be brave little men, and then he escorted them to a car where a nurse and a eugenics officer waited.

"You will go down in history," he told them. "Be proud of your heritage, and when I see you in twenty years you will rule the world."

Naturally, the Twins were confused, but for the journey they had each other, and their bond was a barrier against fear. When Mrs. Rumbaugh returned from Pittsburgh on the streetcar, she was informed of the situation by Peter. She flew into a rage and vowed to get them back.

At about this time Mom turned and stared at the church door like a dog who knows well in advance when it is about to open.

"Are you okay?" I asked.

"Yes," she said, smiling at herself. "Thought I heard a car pulling up. Just making sure no Rumbaughs crash our party, if you know what I mean."

I stood and looked out the window, but there was just the old Mercedes in the drive. "We're okay," I said.

She continued.

Things didn't go well for the Twins. They were separated for the first time in their lives. Abner was sent to live with a wealthy Pittsburgh steel family in Sewickley, and Adolph moved in with an impoverished coal mining family down in

Uniontown. The Twins were fully observed, and the eugenicists hopefully theorized that both boys, no matter their social, family, and environmental circumstances, would rise to the top and thus prove that fitter genes made for superior humans. Nurses were assigned to keep charts on their health, table manners, vocabulary, schoolwork, and desire to be first in their class, first in sports, and more aggressive than other boys around them—especially those who were known to come from inferior Eastern European stock, Mexican mixed races, and Jewish families with less vital genes.

Mrs. Rumbaugh continued to search for them with great effort. She had inherited family money of her own and used it to hire the Pinkerton's Detective Agency.

The Twins were four years old when taken away and nine years old when the detectives tracked them down. They forcibly captured the Twins and returned them to Mrs. Rumbaugh. Peter protested. The ERA tried to convince the courts that the children were legally under its care, but the judge ruled against the association. As for the adopting families, apparently the Twins were so forlorn and lifeless while separated, the families did not protest their leaving.

Mrs. Rumbaugh was so incensed with the father for turning them into a "farm and barn" experiment that she left him and Mount Pleasant and moved the Twins to Pittsburgh. They never saw their father again. Even mention of his name was forbidden. By then many of the Twins' brothers and sisters had moved on, and as far as we know Mrs. Rumbaugh did not encourage them to visit. In some hard way she must have blamed them, too.

By then Peter Rumbaugh's own mother had moved in with him. He doted on her as a good son should. He bought her everything she desired. She also demanded that he never mention his wife's name in front of her or have any relations with women again. He complied and slept on a narrow cot in her bedroom—a room that he personally lined entirely in panels of mink fur. She stayed in that room, in her bed, and he waited on her hand and foot.

When his mother died, Peter lined her coffin with mink as well. She had been a diabetic, and as her circulation declined she lost bits and pieces of limbs—toes at first, then fingers, and then a leg. He preserved her bits as if tanning a hide or taxiderming a specimen and kept the pieces in a case that was constructed like a velvet-lined musical instrument case, perfectly compartmentalized to secure the various physical discards.

While in Pittsburgh the Twins' mother worked as a German language and literature teacher at a private high school. She joined the Friends of Germany Bund in Allegheny County as much to be around other Germans and German culture as to drum up business for her skill as an artisan of mourning jewelry, which she would weave from the hair of deceased loved ones. She also participated in the making of German folk costumes and helped organize German dances and welcoming committees for new immigrants from the Fatherland.

Many of the immigrants told her with concern of the new

Nazi theories on racial superiority and of the laws designed to "cleanse" the German population of unwanted genetic elements—mainly Jews, Gypsies, and mixed-race Communists. Although she agreed that good German boys should marry good German girls and have good German children, she had no interest in allowing the Twins to marry anyone. They belonged to her, and she was German enough.

And maybe, just maybe, my mother speculated, she had figured out the Rumbaugh curse and decided to put an end to it—to keep them from marrying and passing the curse to another generation.

To her credit, Mrs. Rumbaugh worked hard and eventually put the boys through college. They were bright and rigorously disciplined, and upon their mother's suggestion became pharmacists. Once they graduated, the three moved back to Mount Pleasant, took a bank loan, and constructed the Rumbaugh Pharmacy Building on Main Street. The boys steadily nurtured the business, remained loyal to their mother, and like their father and grandfather, became interested in embalming, tanning, and taxidermy.

All those years, my mother said, their mother continued to dominate them, forbidding them to marry, or even date. The boys stayed in check, and she lived on. The only spot of trouble they got into was when they misjudged a prescription—sending a strong diuretic medication to a patient suffering from chronic diarrhea, which resulted in rapid dehydration and near death. The Twins were sued by the patient's family, but in court each Twin testified that he did not fill the prescription and that it must have been the other. Since one of them could not specifically be found guilty, they were both released.

"Believe me," Mom said emphatically, "they would remember this testimony trick for later."

She paused here and seemed to sink into herself for a rest, like a motor idling for a moment before taking off again.

While the Twins were growing up with their mother, she continued, it was found out that their father, Peter Rumbaugh, had traveled to Germany with a delegation of eugenics association members for a seminar at Frankfurt's Institute for Hereditary Biology and Racial Hygiene. Dr. Otmar von Verschuer himself, a real Nazi thinker, delivered the seminar, accompanied by his assistant and former student Dr. Josef Mengele—the same Mengele who did all those horrid medical experiments on people in the death camps. When Peter returned to the United States, he even endorsed a petition presented to the mayor of Mount Pleasant that the poor be limited in the number of children they could produce while the rich were encouraged to breed more freely.

I must have appeared shocked, because Mom looked at me and said, "It's even hard for me to imagine, but back then people were *imagining* a different world."

Already the eugenics society had begun to influence the laws of the country at the highest level. Supreme Court Justice Oliver Wendell Holmes, in the majority decision for the forced sterilization of a "feebleminded" woman, Carrie Buck, wrote that "three generations of imbeciles are enough." This basically meant that sixty thousand "unfit" women who lived in poverty, or in ignorance, or who were mentally ill or just epileptic were sterilized across the country. Plus, immigration policy was influenced by which cultures were judged to have superior genes. Most were Europeans, of course—except for the Jews, who were limited in immigrating to the United States so were trapped in Germany to await Hitler's Final Solution (Hitler is said to have called Grant's *Passing of the Great Race* his "Bible").

Years later, after the horrors of the death camps were exposed, some U.S. eugenicists were writing letters of recommendation for death camp scientists to come and teach at U.S. universities. It seems the Nazi scientists—especially Dr. Mengele, who specialized in twins—did a lot of research on hereditary traits. The eugenicists wanted his research conclusions to help advance their cause, but his scientific files disappeared after the war. That wasn't all that disappeared. Of the 3,000 twins Dr. Mengele worked on, only 157 are known to have survived.

"It's a bit ironic," my mother said, as she finished up, "that a lot of Rumbaughs fought and died in both World Wars One and Two—American Germans fighting European Germans over racial superiority, when both countries shared many of the same race policies."

A PLOT OF HER OWN

The church remained damp, and as the sun was still shining after my mother's talk, we stood and walked outside. "I have a few more things to clear up for you," Mom said, leading me by the hand across the soggy, slumping grass bays between the tombstones. "And for this bit of news I think you'll need to brace yourself."

I had always thought there would be an unmistakable line drawn between my childhood and adult life, like a red velvet rope that cordoned off one from the other, and once I passed beyond the rope I figured my past would be set forever like something dead and taxidermed—fixed. What I hadn't anticipated was that there would be no solid ground to the present other than each stirring second that ticked off the clock like a log rolling in water. This left only the future landscape, which seemed vast and full of guesswork. *It has happened,* I thought as she told me to brace myself. *This is the moment when I stop being afraid of the unknown in my childhood and start to be afraid of the unknown in my adult life.*

I didn't know if I was ready to be an adult, and as I held her hand I said, "Sister Nancy always says there are some mysteries that are better left unsolved."

"That may be true when dealing with religion," Mom replied, "but not in this case. You have to know that you are a Rumbaugh. But not just any old Rumbaugh. You are a Rumbaugh with a preexisting condition. You are either Abner or Adolph's daughter."

I stopped moving and felt something slip into place within me, as if an empty chamber was suddenly filled. But was it the chamber of a gun, and did what I now knew make me more dangerous to others? Or was it a chamber within my heart that now made me more dangerous to myself? I didn't know which, and how could I when the answer was so far removed from the question?

And now she had told me I was a Rumbaugh—not just any Rumbaugh but either Abner's or Adolph's daughter.

"Either?" I repeated.

"Either," she replied.

"You might as well tell me the rest," I said, a bit dazed and wondering how we would work together on clearing up the mystery of *either.*

"Let's walk and talk," she suggested. "It will be easier for me." She pointed to a row of squat granite tombstones, each a base for a large oxidized copper angel bowing with hands set firm in prayer, her guardian wings spread wide under the sun.

"You'll notice," Mom said, casually pointing at the stones, "there seems to be an unusual number of mothers buried side by side with sons—even when you look out at the cousins."

I looked down the row of stones, and she was right. There seemed to be mothers and sons buried side by side, with the other children clumped together by themselves. I guessed some had the curse and some didn't.

"Follow me," Mom said, waving me forward. We came to a plain granite stone the width of a headboard for a king-size bed. The name IVY L. RUMBAUGH was carved beneath the word MOTHER into the middle of the stone, with her birth and death dates beneath her name. Then beneath the dates was a carved scroll with the words in script *Eternal Love*. To one side was Abner's name; to the other, Adolph's. Their dates were left blank.

Of course I noticed her name: Ivy. Before this, I knew her only as Mrs. Rumbaugh.

"They insisted on naming you after their mother," Mom said as we both stared down at the ground with firm chins and denouncing eyes, like two old Puritans who could see through the soil and into the empty casket where the devil had done some mischief.

"How did you become pregnant by *either* of them?" I asked. I was utterly confused.

"It bothered me," she started, "that I could get the boys to warm up to me only when they were without their mother. In the morning I greeted them cheerily, with a *Good morning, Abner* and *Good morning, Adolph,* and if their mother was still upstairs preparing her harsh public face, they would blush and grandly kiss my hand as if they were knights from King Arthur's Round Table. They were very boyish, and I don't think they knew the least bit about women. I'd make them coffee, and they would say it was the best they had ever tasted. If I complimented them on their matching outfits, they would blush until the blood in their cheeks welled and the weight of it tilted their faces forward. At those moments I knew they belonged to me. But as soon as the mother came down from her room, carrying the cash drawer and loudly clearing her throat, they no longer paid me any attention.

"Abner sorted the prescriptions the hospital sent over, and if a person came in with a last name that started with the first half of the alphabet he'd fill it, and if it was the second half, Adolph would. I turned on any display lights, checked the ice cream stock in the freezer, checked the mousetraps, put the floor mat out front, and swept the sidewalk. Each time I finished one small task, I looked up at their elevated counter and hoped one of the boys might notice me and say something like 'Good job,' or 'Thank you, June.'

"The compliment that I really deserved and longed for was 'We couldn't do it without you.' It wasn't that I didn't get compliments from my parents at home—they loved me—but I just needed compliments from outside the house. I was growing up, and I wanted the rest of the world to pay attention to my work and appreciate me. But even though the Twins were nice, with that mother around I didn't feel *needed* there, *needed* in the way I was looking for. Sure, I helped them out, but I wanted something more. Something like love, I suppose. But whatever the Twins were capable of revealing about themselves, or showing me, was not inspired by anything I did or said. I suppose most people would just have given up on them, and I would have except I could see how their mother really had them under her thumb, and my resentment toward her made me sympathize with them.

"In some way I felt that they and I shared an unspoken conspiracy against their mother. I also knew that boys will be boys, and so I waited for my time. I'm not the kind to just give up on something. Had I quit trying to warm them up, it would have been more a reflection on my failure than it was a fault of theirs for being such mama's boys.

"I took it upon myself to turn them around, turn them right side out like you would a pair of socks. But nothing seemed to warm them up, and the harder I tried to win them away from their mother the more I was obsessed with them. I thought about them day and night, imagined ways to trick them into having fun. I'd wake up in the morning and bake them braided bread and strudel. I studied German in school and would walk into the pharmacy and read aloud from the German newspaper, searching as I read for a smile or frown on their faces, for some expression or clue to their feelings.

"I was like a smitten puppy around them, constantly performing for their attention and constantly ignored as long as the mother was present. And although when they were alone I could easily get their attention, I realize now what I really wanted was for them to rebel in front of their mother and abandon their loyalty toward her and treat me more adoringly. I wanted to win her sons away. But she was more powerful, and it was maddening to watch them jump whenever she called to them from the back room.

" *'Zwillinge! Zwillinge!'* she'd holler in German. 'Twins! Twins!' Suddenly their ears would twitch like those of startled deer, and they'd drop everything and scramble toward her.

" 'Coming, Mother!' Abner would call out as if answering the call of an angel.

" 'Yes, coming,' Adolph would echo, as he nervously pounded across the wooden floor trying to beat Abner.

"They were too cheap to put a carpet down, and with their hard leather shoes they pounded the oak boards like a gang of Amish carpenters nailing siding on a barn. Even if they were in the midst of a conversation with a customer, they would dash off in midsentence. When they returned, one of them would step in and carry on with their usual brittle efficiency, like spring-driven windup toys.

"I just wanted them to appreciate me. I longed for it. I was at the age when a pat on the back, a hug, a *good job* meant the world to me, and the less chance I had of ever getting one the more I burned for it, and this is how, I think, I went from just trying to get them to appreciate me to flirting with them.

They were old, but because they behaved like boys I guess I responded to them that way.

"One morning I tried on all the lipstick colors, one after the other, wiping one off and sliding another on. 'What do you think?' I'd ask, posing a bit and puckering my lips. 'Like a parrot,' one of them would say just to keep me at bay. I'd try on the blush and mascara. I'd make myself up like a Pittsburgh whore and walk the aisles like a tart. Every now and again, when the mirror was just right, I could catch them peeking at me as I bent over or rolled my hips as I walked. I wasn't entirely innocent because I made sure they knew I was there. They may have been old, but the desire was still in them. Yet they were afraid of their mother. If she had not been around then they would have been far more attentive. But she glared at them, and me, and we all knew that she was the iron hand. I wished about a million times over that she would die.

"After a time I realized that playing games at the pharmacy with two old birds was just a waste of time. I was good in math and had been offered a scholarship to go to a banking trade school for women in Greensburg. I could take the two-year course, work in a bank, and then what? I wasn't sure, but it would be a change.

"And then the mother had a stroke and fell right off her tall stool at the cash register. They carried her up to bed and I never saw her again, although she hung on for some time. I don't think they called a doctor—at least I never saw one. Weeks went by, and the more time they spent camped out by her bedside the more they needed something to help deflect the pain of knowing her time was up. Ab started drinking the medicinal alcohol, and Dolph was doing all he could to fight off his desire for morphine—something he had used for a time after fracturing his ankle from a spill down the cellar stairs. He had set the bones himself. I knew he had also taken to giving his mother shots of morphine because I saw him carrying the loaded syringes up to their apartments.

"On the night they announced her death, I remember feeling something like relief, as if some stumbling block or great pain had been removed from my life. I also felt some guilt. It seemed cruel of me to feel good about the death, and so I tried to suppress my happiness. But inside I was delighted, because I knew for certain that her death would leave the Twins in my hands.

"The funeral parlor was called, and they sent a hearse out to the pharmacy. A few days later there was a service and burial—it was a closed casket, but with her lingering death and all, you expected it to be closed. The Twins were broken up. Most of the time they stayed upstairs in their apartments and I ran the store. They had to come down to fill prescriptions, but other than that and meeting with drug suppliers, they had me do everything.

"This went on through the summer months. They didn't seem to sleep or eat or change their clothes. They really didn't have much to say to me as they went through the motions. I knew they were brokenhearted so I didn't push the personal stuff, and when they went down to the basement to work on their taxidermy, I just left them alone."

She paused and looked at me, and bit down on her lips. "I'm not proud of what happened next, but you have to know."

"At this point," I said, "I need to know. Tell me."

"In the fall," she continued, and bent down to straighten out a little American flag that had fallen out of its VFW holder, "I had to make up my mind about business school in Greensburg. I explained my situation, and when the Twins thought I was leaving, they turned white. And then Ab, or it could have been Dolph, stammered, 'But we need you.' The other one said, 'We'll pay you anything to stay.'

"That's when I figured I had a better opportunity managing the pharmacy, and the thought that I was *needed* really made me feel loyal to them—and the pay improved, too.

"They went through a bad stretch of time, but by Christmas they began to come around. They stopped drinking and using morphine, and it seemed to me that without their mother around they started to grow up some. That was good and bad—bad because they began to have desires like any adult, which confused them. Staying in love with their mother had allowed them to be children forever, and children are entirely self-involved. They didn't want to get married, but they still had those unused adult passions, which turned them into ancient adolescents. And now they wanted their mommy in a different way. After a while they began to follow me about like a puppy. They'd set aside their pharmacy tasks and watch me re-fill the lipstick displays and organize toothbrushes and sort the Greyhound bus tickets we sold.

"Suddenly they were eager to solicit my opinions and be told what to do. They had been entirely dependent on their mother, and without her they needed someone to think for them, and I was more than happy to be that someone. I had watched their mother handle them for so long that I stepped right into her shoes, and soon they were no longer giving me orders but requesting orders. After a time I began to feel as if I was in control. But it was a false sense. I was naïve, and they were using me more than I was using them. I drifted deeper into their world. I was eager to enter—after all, no one had given me an invitation in the past. And so the three of us formed a relationship that seemed as natural as if I were a member of the family. In a way I was. I had become the surro-gate mother, and the pharmacy was turning a healthy profit again. It was my greatest achievement and I was very proud of myself.

"And they thought it was an accomplishment too," Mom said, looking at me. "In an odd gesture they even gave me a cemetery plot in here."

She pointed toward the back rusty iron fence. It bordered a field of untrimmed apple trees that were heavy with small fruit. "It was a peculiar gift, but at the time I thought it was an honor to be given a space in the Rumbaugh cemetery—even if I didn't think I would ever use it, which now I know I will because, with you being a Rumbaugh, I am family. But what really gets to me is even back then they had their eye on me for carrying on that curse. As awful as that mother was, I can respect what she was up to with controlling those boys. I don't think she wanted them to have children. She considered the love curse to be something more than an Oedipal fixation where the sons wanted to kill the father and marry the mother. She thought it was a genetic flaw in the bloodlines, and she wanted to put an end to that. By then the country had state-enforced sterilization to keep the unhealthy from producing unhealthy kids. As far as the mother was concerned the Rumbaugh genes were definitely *unhealthy*."

"But what about their brothers and sisters?" I asked. "They could carry it on."

"Maybe so," she replied, "but as far as I know, Mrs. Rumbaugh never saw her other children again, and she forbade the Twins to contact them because she thought they would be a bad influence. I guess she figured if her kids didn't live with her, then whatever blood curse they had died on the vine.

"But once she died, it opened the door for the Twins to have ideas of their own. After work one day one of the boys asked me upstairs. This caught me off guard because I knew with certainty that since the mother's death no one had been up there. I thought it was another sign of them opening up to me, and so I followed up the back stairs. It was dark. We went down a hallway that was not lit. The streetlamp outside cast just enough yellow light through one of the oculus windows for me to follow his shape toward the front rooms. Finally we went through an open doorway, and he turned on a small wall lamp. I thought the room smelled like medicine. There was a chemical odor drifting through the air, something sweet and cloying, and then he turned and looked at me in a way I had never been looked at before.

"The only words he uttered," my mother said as we reached her plot, "were sadly pathetic. *Please do not talk*, he said, *because I don't know what to say*. He was like an awkward teenager. Then he leaned forward and kissed me, and I kissed him back. It was my first adult kiss and his, too, I thought. I don't know why I thought I was kissing Ab when it just as easily could have been Dolph. I had my eyes closed, and even if they were open it wouldn't have helped with them looking exactly the same. There was a bed in the room, and I fell back onto it and he lay on top of me. We kissed a bit longer, and then he let down his suspenders and lowered his pants, and not wanting to get undressed because it seemed so unseemly, I just pulled my skirt up. He stared to one side while I worked my underclothes off. Then it was over with in less than a couple minutes—it had to be. It was certainly over with before I could adequately figure out how it came to be that I was doing it with him. While it was going on, I just looked away from him, around the room, up at the ceiling, and then I settled my eyes on his backside in the mirror across from us because on his right cheek was a little red scar which attracted me. It was in the shape of a red *A*, and I wondered if it stood for Abner or Adolph. And that bothered me because suddenly I wasn't feeling too proud of myself having just had sex with someone whose name I didn't exactly know."

My mother stopped talking for a moment. She had been speaking hastily, wanting to get through all of this, but now she seemed to run out of breath. Inside she may have returned to a well of shame or pity or anger. She didn't say, but the tears ran down her face. She looked so young to me, like a friend my own age rather than my mother.

"Don't get the idea that this sex was forced," she said, pulling herself back together. "Because it wasn't. I was willing, I just didn't know what I was doing or why. And when it was over with he stood up and put on his pants while I straightened myself up. For a split second we looked at each other with confusion. How did this suddenly happen? For me, the evening had taken an awkward turn that I wanted to get over—like a little spat that you just hash out and then you move on to a better subject. So when he stood up and seemed to share that same confusion, I was relieved and thought the evening would just carry on and we would return to the rest of the work chores.

"I held out my hand for him to hold, and I leaned toward him thinking we might kiss as kind of an ending to the event. But he shuddered and pulled back in horror. He seemed very agitated and asked if I would go home at once because he had to meet his brother who was waiting for him down the hall.

"That's how he put it," Mom said. "That he was meeting

his brother down the hall. At the time it seemed rude that he was going to run down the hall and tell his brother what he had done to me. It made me mad to think of the Twins whispering away like two old crows over what had just happened. It was creepy, too, as if they were in cahoots.

"After he left the room I just stood there. I didn't know why exactly I had had sex with him. Maybe I was just bored. Maybe I thought doing something reckless would change the way I think, would somehow change my small world. Maybe I was so desperate I took a wild chance. Maybe I just wanted to try sex and figured it would be safe with them rather than with some blabbermouth around town. Believe me, it wasn't something well thought out. It was more like mercy sex."

That last line stopped us talking for a minute. She marked off an X on the grass with her foot.

"This is my plot," she said, glancing over each shoulder to make sure of her coordinates. "It's just inside the property line. They shoved me in a corner. I want a little stone with just the name: JUNE SPIRCO. From here I'll have a good vantage point to keep an eye on them."

I wasn't paying any attention to her. I still couldn't get over the phrase *mercy sex*. It seemed so merciless.

"Hold on," I said, raising a hand. "Stop! Finding out the whole story is part of my birthday present. So what happened after the mercy sex? Did you go into the room after him?"

"Yes," she said, reviving. "Absolutely! I got a little huffy and thought I'd straighten that old goat out some. I marched down to the back room, which had been the mother's. I threw open the door, and that's the first time I saw her stuffed. It was quite a shock. He was down on his hands and knees holding her outstretched hand and blubbering like a baby. He was so obsessively contrite with what he had done he had to go kneel before his stuffed mother for a while and hope she would make him feel better for his action. Now I understand, of course, that he never *wanted* sex with me for any other reason than to perpetuate the Rumbaugh curse. It was in his blood to procreate even though it was against her wishes. But he was driven to it.

"The whole thing was revolting! And like you did when you were seven and saw her in the basement, I promised myself I would never go back there again. All the way home I kept telling myself that I would move to Greensburg, beg my way back into the business school, and get the heck out of this freak-show town."

NOT SO FAST

"And like you, I did go back there, but for different reasons," she said. "I was pregnant, and Greensburg went right out the window. I denied my condition at first, but after three months there was no getting around it. I wasn't nauseous, and wasn't showing yet, but I hadn't had a period so I went to the doctor and told him as little as possible about the circumstances. He confirmed my suspicions.

"You can't believe how nervous I was when it came to telling my parents. And really, the worst part wasn't telling them that I was pregnant, but I just knew that when I told them it was by one of the old Rumbaugh twins—and I didn't know which one—they were going to flip.

"And they did. My father was furious. After he called me a few names, he called an attorney and wanted to have them both arrested for statutory rape. But I was eighteen at the time, so I was of age and the sex was consensual. The only issue was of paternity and child support. My attorney wanted to know which one it was. But I didn't know for sure. And of course when the attorney confronted the Twins, they denied it. They were innocent, they claimed. Hadn't laid a glove on me. They even submitted to a blood test, but it was inconclusive. "Well, this is going to be a hard case to win," the attorney said to my father. "Do you want to go through with it?"

"They're grown churchmen," my father reasoned. "They'll tell the truth under oath." I didn't think they would. When my father left the room, I pulled the attorney to one side. There is one thing, I said sheepishly. I told him about seeing the Twin's rear end in the mirror, with the little red *A* scar or tattoo on his right cheek. The attorney wrote that down in a black notebook. I didn't know it then, but country doctors always left some secret scar on identical twins so they could be told apart. Usually they put the scar where people could see it, like behind an earlobe or on an elbow, but for some reason this doctor put it on the rear end.

"Well, before a trial was called there was a probable cause hearing and the Twins were submitted to examination in the judge's chamber. My attorney thought he had an ace up his sleeve because of the scar I had seen. But when they were examined, an *A* was found on each of them—both on the same side!

"I'm sure they somehow worked out a way for the one with the *A* to be examined twice. I remember that they had to keep the drugstore open because of all the hospital needs, and so they were examined one at a time by the judge. And even though there was an *A*, both of them denied doing it, just as they did with that diuretic prescription years back. And once again that trick worked and they were found not responsible for my pregnancy because it couldn't be proven which one it was. Well, the attorney couldn't get any further, and my parents were so embarrassed they planned to move. I knew it would not be good to stay with them. Besides, they were on the verge of sending me to a home for unwed mothers, where you would be taken from me at birth and I would be left with an unwed mother's reputation and no baby to love me. It was the worst situation I could imagine. I didn't have many options, so I sat down and wrote the Twins a letter about what I had seen—not about the *A*—but about seeing their mother and knowing what they had done with her. I was a bit angry and desperate, so desperate I threatened to go to the police if they didn't help me.

"Not long after I sent the letter, Mrs. Ushock showed up at my parents' house. She had some *private business* to conduct, she said sternly. My parents sent me out of the room. I don't know what lies she told them, but when I came back into the room my mother sent me to get my clothes and leave with Mrs. Ushock. 'It will be better this way' was all my dad said.

"Then Mrs. Ushock drove me to the Kelly Hotel, and I was escorted up to these rooms. She examined me on the kitchen table like I was some sort of farm animal. She told me that I would not be going to a doctor or a hospital and that I was to stay in the hotel for the next few months. She told me that she would have my groceries sent up and anything else I needed, and when the time came she alone would be the midwife.

" 'That would be good,' I said. 'But who is going to pay for this?'

"She opened her purse and pulled out an envelope full of papers.

" 'This is a contract,' she said. 'The Rumbaughs will pay for your expenses and will pay for these rooms and for raising the child and all you have to do is keep *the secret*. I suppose the secret refers to which one of them is the father,' she said roughly.

"I let her think that way. But I knew they didn't care about who had done what to me. *The secret* was about what they had done to their mother. I read the papers. Aside from keeping *the secret*, they also stated that I couldn't move from Mount Pleasant or I would forfeit custody of you. Well, of course I couldn't afford to move, and nobody was going to take you away unless it was over my dead body.

"Once I signed the papers, a bank account was set up in my name and every month money was put into it, and it continues to be funded to this day.

"You were born just fine. Mrs. Ushock knew what to do, and afterward I stayed home with you. When you started nursery school I worked some for the Twins, but then I thought it best to move on, and since I always liked true crime I took a course in court stenography and got the courthouse job.

"I had to stay at the hotel. My parents had moved to Florida to retire and pretty much left me on my own. One died before you were born, and the other went before you were out of diapers. They didn't leave any money to speak of, so it helped that the Twins paid a lot of the bills. Also, I wanted to raise you around your father. I know that sounds odd, but I thought that over time one of them would step forward and say he was the one. And although that didn't happen, never in my wildest dreams did I ever think *my baby* would inherit the Rumbaugh curse. When Ab and Dolph and I finally worked through what I knew they had done to their mother and they told me about the family history and the curse, I thought it was too creepy and too unlikely to be real. But I also knew it wasn't entirely a ghost story—plus you were a girl, and as far as I knew no girls had inherited it."

"So which is my father?" I asked.

"It doesn't matter," she said.

"It does to me," I replied. "It didn't before, but after all this I want to know."

"Either will do," she said airily.

"What do you mean, *either*?"

"They're identical twins, hon. They're the same. Same blood. Same genes. Same freakish behavior. So either will do."

"It's not like picking a can of peas off a shelf," I insisted. "Now tell me, which one is my father?"

"Well, I honestly don't know. The only hint I can give you is that your father has a red *A* scar on his right rear cheek. I know that for a fact, though neither one of them has ever owned up to which one has it."

"Then I'll find out," I said.

"What will you do? Just ask them to pull down their pants?"

"That would be a good start," I replied.

"I already tried that once and it didn't work."

"Then I'll think of something," I said. "Now that you've told me this much, I have to know."

"More important than knowing," she said, "is this. You have to get out of here. Leave this town. Had I gone to Greensburg as I planned, none of this would have happened. Don't get me wrong, I couldn't live without you and you've meant everything to me, but I don't want you to become a victim of this Rumbaugh curse."

"Don't be ridiculous," I said. "I'm not going to do to you what they did to their mother."

"Cross your heart?"

I crossed my heart, but as I did so I could feel a chamber in my heart pumping Rumbaugh blood through me with a crossed purpose. I adored my mother, and if I was lying to her, I reasoned I was doing so for her own good.

And then to get away from all this talk Mom pulled a little box out of her purse. She placed it in my hands.

"Happy birthday," she said. "Open it. This is how you should remember me—the old-fashioned way."

I untied the ribbon, lifted the lid, and parted the tissue paper. Inside was a gold heart-shaped locket on a gold chain. She held the box and I opened the locket. It was a picture of her smiling out at me. I put it around my neck, and she fastened the clasp. I turned and smiled and could see that she was happy and convinced that her nurturing was stronger than my nature.

"I have something for you, too," I said. "It's an odd present because it's something that is yours but you can't own it." I unbuttoned my blouse and pulled back the left side, then with my thumb tugged my bra down across my breast. Against my white skin was a solid red tattoo of a heart. A scroll across the top read: MOTHER. A scroll below read: ETERNAL LOVE.

She was shocked. "When did you get that?" she asked, as if it were something I had stolen.

"Last week," I said quietly, feeling a bit dejected by her reaction. "I went up to the tattoo parlor and got it for you. I had no idea it was the same as on the tombstone."

"Ivy," she said, shaken, "if I had told you this story about your background years ago, do you think it would have made a difference about how you are now? I mean, with your interest in taxidermy and the pharmacy and now this?" She pointed at my chest.

"You don't mean the tattoo," I said. "You mean me. How I feel about you."

"Yes," she said.

"First, I don't think that loving you is a curse," I said. "I love you and I will always love you desperately and there is nothing wrong with that. You can say it's in my blood, and I'd have to agree with you because it is a daughter's destiny to love her mother. And I love you with all my heart." These words came out without my having to think of them because they were always in me. They were part of my nature.

Far above us, another nature was also being itself. While we were in the cemetery the weather had shifted. In the middle of the gray sky a black cloud gathered, and below it the ground became strangely dark. I stared up at its jagged underside which was as carved out and rugged as the bottom of an iceberg. Suddenly the wind dropped straight down against my face and a cold rain began to fall. Flecks of ice followed and stung like tiny needles. In an instant the cloud began to descend directly upon us, and we ran for the caretaker's shed at the edge of the property. The trapped wind pressed down on my head and shoulders with the force of a heavy hand. I could barely lift my feet to run. The flecks of ice turned into beads of hail, then larger, and then they hurt. We struggled forward, pulling ourselves along gravestone by gravestone until we made it to the shed door.

"Stay away from the windows!" my mother ordered as we dashed inside. We stood in the middle of the shed and held on to each other as the building roared from the pummeling of the hail against the tin roof.

"Is it a tornado?" I asked.

"No," she said. "Just a sudden storm, a microburst, where the cold air drops straight down. It's rare, but it happens."

"I'm afraid," I said, and held her tightly.

"I'm more afraid of something else," she said. "Promise me you will leave here and go to school like I should have done and get away from the Twins. Their mother thought she put an end to this curse, but she didn't. Once she died, they did what was in them to do. But I'll put an end to it. You leave. You'll go to college—to Seton Hill for religious training. Sister Nancy says you have a calling for it. Promise me. Until then, never let them lay a hand on you," my mother said desperately. "They are driven to keep the curse alive, and I don't want them thinking you are a link in their genetic chain."

It was a curse that I loved my mother so much I had to obey her. "Yes, I promise," I said without sensing any lie. "I'll go away."

Then the roaring stopped. Some stray hail ticked across the roof. Then it was all clear. We let go of each other. The shed smelled of gasoline and cut grass. I opened the door, and the fresh air reached in like a cool hand.

"Oh, it's awful," my mother said, looking out at the cemetery and the misty white sea of hail. Shattered apple tree branches were strewn about like the limbs of soldiers that Hermann Rumbaugh must have witnessed after a battle. I bent down and dug out a split apple and could imagine Hermann and his crew of body pickers searching across the vast carnage of a battlefield, uncurling fingers for rings they could cut off in order to read the names stamped inside the bands.

I looked over at my mother, who was pointing toward Ab

and Dolph's car. It looked like a madman had obsessively attacked it with a hammer. Every inch was dented like the dimpled surface of a golf ball. The windshield was cratered like a glass moon.

"Good Lord," she said, laughing. "For once Mother Nature has given them a beating." And she continued to laugh too hard and too loud until it was obvious that she was not laughing at the car. It was a deeper laugh, as if unburdening herself of her past had caused a microburst of relief. She laughed until she bent over, crooked and stiff with her hands on her knees.

I stared down at her, and from that moment on I thought of my mother as the child and myself as the adult. I felt not older but only that it was I who had to protect her and not the other way around. This was the line I crossed when I left my childhood to become an adult.

I rubbed her back and helped straighten her up, and we silently struggled arm in arm across the ice, then stood by the side of the road until a farmer's wife gave us a ride into town.

3
NINE YEARS EARLIER

Freaks are a fairy tale for grownups.
—Diane Arbus

SQUIRRELS ARE MY FAVORITE

It had taken until I was sixteen for me to hear the other side of the story, the *alteram partem*, as Mother had put it. Until then it had been inappropriate for her to tell me everything I wanted to know because I was young and because she wanted to protect me from what all Mrs. Ushock knew. And I suspect she wished to believe that my love for her was pure and not provoked by a dreadful curse in the way the Twins' love was toward their mother, and Peter Rumbaugh's and Hermann Rumbaugh's was toward their mothers, and who knows how far back in time the love curse went—maybe all the way back to some dark forest in Germany.

For my mother to tell me that my love for her was partially an artificial love, like a love generated by a genetic disease, or a hypnotic fraud, must have taken a lot of courage. And in realizing just how courageous she was to tell me the truth about her past and mine, I have come to love her all the more. It is not perfection that captures the heart but honesty.

But when I was seven I did not know any of this Rumbaugh history and curse, which I now know is my history and curse, too. In hindsight I can comment on those early years—from the moment I saw the stuffed mother until I turned sixteen. I can try to explain them to you in a deeper way than if I revealed them as I lived them, for then I was blinded by so many things that were overpowering me.

For instance, strange things began to happen to me immediately after I tried to mount my rag doll in the hotel bathroom. Right after Mrs. Kelly found it and caused my mother to worry about me, I woke up so odd to myself, so confused by my strange compulsive behavior that the only peace for me was to give in to impulses I could not control.

I was ready to hear Ab and Dolph's side of the story about their stuffed mother, only it turned out that uncovering the whole story of the Twins' other side was like journeying into a Black Forest fairy tale that grew more puzzling and disturbing the deeper I ventured into its murky shadows. After I had run up the stairs that Easter Sunday morning, screaming that I had seen Mrs. Rumbaugh and scaring the life out of the Twins, they surely wanted to do everything possible to go to the grave with their secrets. But after those few days away from them, I just as surely wanted their secrets before they went to the grave. I needed to know about their relationship with their mother and why and how they preserved her, and I wanted to know how it was that at seven years old I felt the same urge to preserve my own mother. I wanted them to answer that question, so after school, as I told my mother I would, I returned to the pharmacy.

"I'm back!" I announced, marching through the front door with a determined look on my face. The Twins were standing behind their tall rear counter while bottling pills.

For a frozen moment they stared down at me like two old parsnips, then wordlessly returned to their work.

"I want to go downstairs," I said forcefully.

"Ab and I agreed that's off-limits now," Dolph replied, jerking his thumb toward the basement door, which was further protected with a new hasp and lock. "No more playing in the cottage area. We had a burst pipe that ruined it down there."

"I don't want to play in my cottage," I said. "I want to play in your workshop where you stuff the animals."

"Why?" Ab asked, quizzing me.

"I want to stuff animals for a hobby," I replied. "And I want you to teach me everything you know."

"You're not old enough," Ab insisted, crossing his arms over his chest.

"It's too gruesome for a girl," Dolph added. "Boys only."

I pulled over the step stool so I could climb up and look them in the eye. Then I said something that was entirely unrehearsed. Although I didn't know it, it was the same instinctive threat my mother had used so many years before. "If you don't let me back down there and teach me what you know, I'll tell the police what I saw," I said evenly.

Ab abruptly turned his back on me and said to Dolph with concern in his voice, "Seems to me she favors her mother's kin."

"The same threat," Dolph said, swallowing rapidly.

"Did your mother put you up to this?" Ab suddenly asked as he whirled around toward me like an inquisitor.

"Of course not," I replied. "It's my idea. She wouldn't like it."

A look of satisfaction settled onto Ab's face as he turned to Dolph. "Maybe she is more like us," he said.

"But she's a *girl*," Dolph replied suspiciously.

"It's the *blood*," Ab said wisely. "It's more genes than gender."

"Hmm," Dolph concluded, and nodded his head in agreement. "After all, she came back, and that would be the sign of her affliction."

"The curse," Ab said, proudly looking up at the photograph of his mother. "She comes by it honestly."

Apparently, after I had seen their mother that Easter morning, they had debated whether I would return. The curse had always shown up in the men, and although they knew I was part Rumbaugh, they were not sure how much I would follow their family path, or my mother's. But I surprised them with just how much Rumbaugh blood had infected me.

"I need to know how to preserve things," I said.

"We'll help with animals but nothing beyond that," Dolph replied, turning toward me.

"And you'll need a specimen," Ab added.

"I brought one." I had a brown grocery bag and pulled out my misshapen rag doll, which I'd saved from the trash.

"That's a toy," Ab said, carefully taking it from me and flipping it all about as if examining a newborn. "You need a real specimen."

"Can you get me one?" I asked.

"That can be arranged," Ab said. Then he stuck out his hand to shake, as did Dolph.

"It's a deal," I agreed, and placed my small hand between theirs as if it were a key that perfectly fit between the teeth of a lock.

It was from that moment on the Twins were convinced that the hereditary Rumbaugh curse was in my blood and that preserving my mother was not some perverse child's game or an idea thrust upon me from a horror film. They began to groom me to stay forever true to the Rumbaugh legacy, and my apprenticeship as a junior taxidermist began.

Each day after school they gave me a lesson. We started small.

Squirrels were easy to manage. I learned to slice the fur from the flesh without nicking their delicate features. The Twins showed me where to make the key incisions along the underside of the body, from the tail up to the chin, and how to branch off from this central divide and slice down the arms and legs. They trained me how to slowly tug the skin with one hand while simultaneously slicing away the underlying adhesive membrane with the other, as if removing the peel from a grape. After the skin was slowly detached, they taught me how to bathe and preserve it in a solution of alum and salt. The flesh and eyes were removed with a variety of sharp, curved knives while the bones, tendons, and claws were kept for strength and shape. Once that step was complete and after the skeleton had fully dried, they instructed me how to gently return the pliable skin back over the skull and then partially sew up the body with neat, small glove stitches. As the body took shape, they showed me how to use a forceps to stuff the squirrel with nonshrinking sculptor's clay and cotton batting in order to give it shape, and because the clay didn't dry right away after I had fully stuffed and sutured the squirrel back up, I could pat and pinch and squeeze the skin in order to position the clay and cotton so that all the muscles were in the correct proportions. The eyes were ordered from a taxidermy supply house, as were extra teeth, and they were all glued in.

Each day I worked on my squirrel bodies. When I finished one, Ab or Dolph would go over it with me and point out what I did right or wrong and how I could remedy the problems. And if I messed up too badly, then one of the Twins would take the .22 squirrel rifle out to the edge of town and I'd have a fresh specimen the next day.

When Mother arrived from work on the bus I'd show her

my projects, and she would awkwardly smile down on me, and Ab and Dolph would proudly tell her that I was a natural at the art. They'd make a big fuss over me, and they were smart enough to make a fuss over her, too. They'd get her a black marble mortar bowl of ice cream and a cold bottle of Coke and give her all the makeup samples they had received and anything else she wanted—all for free. They wanted to keep me firmly under their control, but at the same time they didn't want Mother to feel left out. They even gave her driving lessons and encouraged her to use their Mercedes. Of course, the more she used the car, the more time I spent with the Twins.

Within six months I had progressed so well that I wanted to mount my squirrels. At first I did the typical poses. Squirrel on a stump with a prized acorn in hand. Spooked squirrel on the side of a tree limb with its head cocked toward some danger. Squirrel in a tree hole with its cute little head sticking out. But after a while I lost interest. Preserving them was all about technique and making them look authentic. If I wanted to see a squirrel, I could just step outside and see them in the trees, so there was no imagination involved.

"I'm bored stiff," I said to Ab.

"What do you have in mind?" he replied.

"I'm not quite sure," I said, "but I'll give it some thought."

"You better hurry," he advised. "We have a taxidermy show and contest over in York next month, and I think it's time you enter the junior category."

That night over dinner I asked Mom what I should do.

"They used to take me to those contests," she recalled hesitantly.

"So, what did you see?" I asked eagerly.

"Well, the examples I remember best always seem to tell a story," she said. "A fish that just looks like a fish is pretty dull. That's why the good taxidermists show a fish struggling to be caught—you can imagine the moment. Or they show a bird feeding its young. Or butterflies swirling around an orchid. In other words, they breathe a little life into the scene. And in a way you end up caring about it and kind of get away from being creeped out that you are staring at something that was once alive."

Tell a story. Breathe some life into it. That gave me some ideas.

The next day I began to work out a plan. I had a squirrel Cinderella scrubbing the floor with her very own tears under the caption CINDERELLA WEEPS FOR HER MOTHER. In a few days I had fixed the position of the squirrel, but I needed the Twins to help me with the other details.

In a month we were ready. Cinderella was kneeling on the floor wearing an old gray smock, dirty apron, and gingham mobcap. They had helped me sew the clothes. She had a scrub brush in one hand that we made out of the painted head of a child's toothbrush. Dried Super Glue tears were dripping from her eyes, and a puddle gathered below. I could really *feel* her broken heart as she missed her mother. We constructed a little wooden bucket out of split twigs, and I painted the backdrop with a fireplace, because she got her name from cleaning up fireplace cinders. I wanted to be accurate.

Ab and Dolph helped me set it into a glass case, and they painted the title in gold script just as they did for their other displays.

For their entry they had produced the classic twin scene of Narcissus falling in love with his reflection. They used a black snake coiled up and entranced with himself as he stared down into a watery blue mirror.

I had kept the Cinderella project a secret from my mother until just before the contest. When I unveiled my display she praised it, but when the Twins left the room she took me aside.

"I don't want to discourage you," she said carefully, and smoothed my hair with her hand as if soothing me. "But I don't want you to get carried away with all this *morbid* taxidermy."

"Are you worried that I did a lost mother scene?" I asked.

"Yes," she frankly replied. "I'm just thinking of how upset you got at school not so long ago."

"Please don't worry," I said. "Ever since I've started this I've felt so much better. I'm really happy."

"Okay," she said.

But she wasn't okay.

Looking back on this time, I can see how hard it must have been for her. On the one hand, if I stayed away from the Twins

I just got myself worked up at school and had terrible anxiety thinking that something horrid was going to happen to her. On the other hand, when I was with the Twins she began to see that my interest in taxidermy and my devotional love for her were somehow tied to the Rumbaugh curse. She wanted me to remain happy, so she let me work with them, but she continuously kept a watchful eye on me. She knew she was walking a fine line; still, she felt confident that while I was young her influence over me was greater than theirs. I'm not trying to second-guess her, because I would have done the same if I were in her shoes.

At the York taxidermy show, the Twins and I received honorable mentions in the general competition and runner-up red ribbons in the Animal Animation category. When we returned to the pharmacy, they displayed my Cinderella diorama on the top of one of the shelves. And anytime a customer came in, they'd quickly point it out and make a big fuss over me. "She's the best of the bunch of us" was what they would say.

I was so proud, and my success encouraged me.

All of my following subjects had something to do with a missing mother. I did a medley, from a kitten Snow White under glass with an acid green crab apple in her mouth to a *Little Mermaid* scene where Ariel searches for her dead mother, to Bambi's mother being shot by the hunter. I didn't always have the right animals—for instance, I didn't have a real mermaid, so I lacquered a sea horse, glued on the hair, and painted the face and tail. It looked a little odd but the idea was good. I used a rabbit for Bambi's mom and just trimmed the ears back with scissors so she appeared more like a deer.

The Twins also enjoyed taking twin scenes from literature. They did THE PRINCE AND THE PAUPER, which they illustrated with baby pigs, and DR. JEKYLL AND MR. HYDE, using a fox cub for the gentleman doctor and a raging wild boar for his alter ego. They did a great Tweedledum and Tweedledee out of penguins, which they had shipped up in dry ice from southern Chile, and a creepy scene out of raccoons where Louis XIV visits his twin brother in the Bastille from *The Man in the Iron Mask*. I thought they were brilliant, and they won gold ribbons wherever they were displayed.

As I improved I won medals as well. I did Nancy Drew and Little Orphan Annie and Dorothy from *The Wizard of Oz*. It seemed there was no end to finding kids with dead mothers or missing mothers in literature. And the more I realized that so many young girls were without their mothers, the more I clung to mine.

And she clung to me. Each night, as soon as she arrived at the pharmacy, I put down my taxidermy project and thought of nothing else but her. We'd leave the Twins behind and go over to the Kelly Hotel and enter our own world, where she had set our own family rules.

"Rule number one," she had insisted. "No taxidermy talk and no dead mother talk. That kind of talk is just double trouble. I want a normal life here. Girl talk. Mother-daughter talk. This is the *fun* side of the street. And that," she said, pointing directly out our window at the pharmacy, "is the *funky* side of the street."

It never mattered what she said, I always agreed with her entirely, and so we had fun. We went to movies. We bowled. We had manicures. We went shopping. We went to the park and played. We went out for cheap dinners. It was just us, and when we were alone her influence over me was magnetic and I stayed by her side and all was right with the world.

I didn't mind not talking about taxidermy, and my worries over her death subsided because we were so alive then, cooking and getting dressed up and taking photographs of each other and talking and playing music and singing into a tape recorder and dancing and squealing like girls and in bed we would lie side by side and I would read a chapter that she would tape and the next night she would read a chapter and I would tape it. Of course, in some way, I knew I was taping her voice for a special reason, but the fun of doing so concealed the stealthy motive for doing it.

And she made sure I did a lot of things any normal kid would do—I went to dozens of birthday parties, had plenty of sleepovers, participated in just about every church event, from bazaars and charity banquets to community service and Bible camp. I started and quit piano lessons, violin lessons, flute lessons, gymnastics, and tap and ballet. We didn't bother with sports, and because of my taxidermy interest we avoided getting a dog or cat or fish or even a hermit crab for a pet. My mother was pretty sure it would just end up as a specimen.

As I grew older I did not rebel against her. Instead, I rebelled against my own nature. I resented growing up. After a while I couldn't jump into her arms or sleep curled up like a little moon-faced cameo around her belly, or stand on her feet and clutch her legs as we danced across the kitchen. My shoes got longer. Clothes would fit, and then before I knew it they would bind up around my shoulders and hips until I was no longer loose inside them. I was a long-limbed snake constantly molting from one outfit to another, and I didn't like it. I wanted to remain her little girl, her sparkling pinkie ring, her shiny plastic toy.

Without knowing how or why, I felt my Rumbaugh curse was going to be the death of my mother despite my desire to keep her alive. When I asked myself why I felt this way, or thought this way, I didn't have a sensible answer. I just *did*. It was a mark upon me.

So the question is, was my fear of her death caused by nature or nurture? Was it in my Rumbaugh genes, as Mom told me later, or was it only as I thought at the time—that I was a young girl who loved her mother and feared her death? No girl wants her mother to die, so fearing her loss doesn't seem excessive. Plus, my sadness from indulging in thoughts of her death while I worked on the taxidermy was gloriously contrasted by how overjoyed I was when she came home from work and I threw myself into her arms. It was as though, each day, she was resurrected to save just me, and this was very pleasurable.

But lurking behind this ticking clock of fear and joy was the unspoken dread that someday she was not going to come home and I would have to do what the Twins did. I couldn't predict the future. All I could predict was that the future would arrive and I would have to be prepared.

THE CABINET

Years ago, right after I had seen the stuffed mother for the first time that Easter morning, my mother asked me how many Mrs. Rumbaughs I had seen. At that moment my mind was too full of the one I *had* seen to even consider the question. But over time the question never quite dissolved either, and when I asked my mom about it, she just shrugged it off as if she'd only been checking up on my eyesight. It didn't seem like an issue to her, so I never pushed it until one day I was in the basement.

I was twelve. It was a Sunday after church and bitter cold. For weeks an arctic low-pressure system had nestled into the valleys between the mountains. The ground was frozen solid. Frost heaves turned the roads into chunky vertebrae of asphalt. The rivers were gray and hard as solder. Usually, Mother and I met up with the Twins for some refreshments at the pharmacy, but they were at a prescription insurance seminar in Pittsburgh. Mom wasn't feeling well. She had come down with a cold and after church had crawled back into bed to take a nap. I told her I would go over to the pharmacy and get her some aspirin and cold tablets. "Hurry back," she said as she gave me the key to the front door. "Don't go down into the basement and get carried away with your work."

"Okay," I replied, but as I left the room I already knew I wanted to do a few other things while I was there. I had been spending a lot of extra time piecing together a scene illustrating the 1917 sighting of the Virgin of Fatima in Portugal, which I was going to donate for the church raffle. Three young shepherds had seen the Virgin, and I had taxidermed little golden finches to represent them, but the delicate image of the mist-shrouded Virgin was tricky to capture. I tried a piece of painted glass, but it seemed too clunky for a vision. I thought a hologram might be best, but I couldn't find one. Finally, I settled on a phosphorescent butterfly, which I had ordered through a catalog. But for it to hang properly, I needed to lightly spray the body with a urethane fixative before painting on her robes. This was on my mind as I dashed out of the Kelly Hotel and into the cold. I figured if I hurried I could apply a quick coat before coming back with the medicine.

I crossed the street, and when I arrived I saw that the door was slightly ajar. I pushed it open with my foot, and a wave of warm air passed over me. "Ab?" I cautiously called out. "Dolph?" I closed the door behind me and pulled off my gloves. I figured they hadn't closed the door properly and were either upstairs or down in the basement.

I walked into the shop and quickly put a bottle of aspirin and some cold tablets into my jacket pocket. Because the heat was on, I figured the spray fix would work even better on the butterfly, so I turned toward the basement. That was when I noticed the hasp and lock had been pried off the door. Maybe Ab and Dolph had lost the key and had to pry it open, I thought. Still, I was suspicious, and a little afraid. But the cash drawer was kept downstairs in the drug room with the week's receipts, so I got up my courage and opened the basement door. I didn't want to upset Mom unless something truly was wrong.

The stairwell light was on.

"Hello!" I called down. There was no reply. I listened intently for any sounds. If I heard anything, I could dash out the door. But all was quiet. Then I descended the stairs backward so that if someone was down there I'd be facing the right way to scamper up ahead of them. About halfway down I could see that the rear basement light was also on. I took a deep breath. "Hello!" I called out. Again I received no answer. When I reached the last step, I quickly dashed to my right and slipped into the dark taxidermy workroom. I stood still, and after a minute my eyes adjusted and I could see that the room had not been disturbed. I peeked out of the door crack toward the back side of the basement, where my old cottage used to be and where the Twins had the locked wire drug cage. After a few minutes I didn't hear any sounds or see anyone.

I stepped into the light and tiptoed to the stairwell and again called out toward the drug cage. "Hello!" There was no response, and as I stood there I could make out that the wire door to the drug room had been buckled open with a crowbar that was left on the floor. *A burglar*, I thought, and now I was really afraid that the cash was stolen.

"Hello!" I shouted again. I couldn't see anyone, and even though I wanted to run home, I needed to know about the money. I took one silent step after another, picking my way around discarded bottles of pills until I reached the drug room. I retrieved the crowbar and held it like a baseball bat just in case, but no one was there. The burglary was over with. A few boxes of drugs were ripped open, and bottles were scattered across the floor. I had a suspicion it was the same burglar as before, and because he never seemed too dangerous, I felt a little less afraid. I figured he took what pills he wanted and left. Then I glanced over at the wooden cabinet where the Twins kept the cash drawer. They always kept it locked.

But this time it was partway open, and whoever had looked inside must have gotten a fright, because I did. In a panic to find out about the money I flung open the cabinet door, and when I saw that *face* I jumped back and screamed. Right in the center of the first shelf was their mother's detached head—the same one I had seen when I was seven. She still had those slightly glowing eyes and that sewn-together mouth, which gave her a tight-lipped smile. She was wearing a curly black wig pinned to her head.

I had run the first time I saw her, but after a good scream

the second time I pulled myself together. After all my taxidermy experience she seemed more of a specimen than a spook. Now I was curious. Why was the head here? Right away I could see that her face had cured badly, and there was a lot of crazing where the skin was pulled too tightly over the raised brows and cheekbones, and around the entire chin. One of the Twins had rubbed saddle soap into her skin to keep it from cracking open. I could smell it as I carefully lifted her from the shelf. She was heavy. I wondered what material they had used to fill in the brain cavity. I raised her up over my head to peer into the neck, but it was solid plaster except for a hole just big enough to slip onto a wooden dowel.

I set her down on top of the cabinet and looked inside. There was a stack of drawers, and I opened the one where the money was always kept. It was safe. The burglar must have seen the head and run for the hills, and the thought of his screaming and scampering wildly up the stairs made me smile a bit with remembering how I had felt years before.

Since there were other drawers, I knew I had to open them. This might be my only chance. In the first one there was a lot of old jewelry that must have belonged to their mother. I opened another drawer and jerked back. It was filled with egg-shaped prosthetic eyes, and as they waddled back and forth and clicked together they stared out at me with trapped, insane expressions. I slammed shut the drawer as if it were incubating some abnormal creation and opened the next.

There was an old black plastic compact with a mirror, a

bottle of flesh-colored nail polish, a package of false eyelashes, and bobby pins. Nothing of special interest.

Finally, I checked the last drawer. Inside were two human hands. Where the wrist ended a dowel stuck out, and I guessed the hands on the mother were interchangeable so the Twins could alter the poses. One was closed into a loose fist, as if it could hold an umbrella, or flyswatter. The other was more open, with the fingers curled up a bit for carrying a purse. I distinctly remembered seeing hands on the mother and wondered if these were the same hands, or did the Twins have extras? And if so, how?

I had to find out. I backtracked upstairs to the pharmacy, then behind the counter and up the rear stairs to the hall that bisected Ab's and Dolph's identical apartments. I had not seen the mother since that Easter morning when I was seven, and it gave me the creeps to check their apartments because I knew when I saw her body again it would have an effect over me. But I was prepared for that sight.

What I didn't expect was finding the same body but with a different head. I walked into Ab's living room, and there she was with a head carved out of wood and painted brightly like the Nutcracker. You would think I would have screamed and jumped back. But it wasn't like that at all. It was surprising, but in a good way, like when you open a birthday gift and get the doll you have been asking for. I stood there and looked at her and smiled, and right away I wanted to play with her. I stepped behind her and carefully lifted her head with both my hands. It was just as I thought: the heads were interchangeable. Also, the arms could be adjusted back and forth at the shoulders, and when I checked the hands, I saw that they too were removable. Without thinking, I slipped right into doll talk.

"Hello, Ivy," I said, speaking for her in what I thought would be a German-sounding voice, "how lovely to meet you."

"And you," I replied and did a quick curtsy.

"Could you get me a scarf?" she said. "My neck is cold."

"Yes, Mrs. Rumbaugh," I replied. There was a man's scarf draped over the back of a chair, and I reached for it and arranged it around her neck.

"Thank you," she said.

And then I guessed I was going to find something else in Dolph's apartment. "Excuse me for a moment," I said as politely as I could. "I'll be right back."

I walked over to Dolph's door and opened it and found exactly what I expected. The second mother was sitting down, headless, in an overstuffed chair, knitting. Just above the neck of her dress was a four-inch wooden dowel where the head would fit—the head they were repairing downstairs. There was a cup of cold tea on the side table next to her, and the radio quietly broadcast one of Bach's Sunday cantatas.

At that moment many different responses could have overwhelmed me. I could have been revolted, or spooked, or even gotten sick, but instead the strongest feeling I had was jeal-

ousy. It was the most amazing sensation, and entirely unexpected. I was jealous! I wanted one, too—one of these big
dolls. And then I realized that the Twins must have been jealous of each other, because there was only one mom and there
were two of them. And so they came up with a solution. But
just how did they get two moms from one body?

They must have sawed her in half somehow, I guessed. After
I checked the moms over, going back and forth between the
rooms and looking under their clothes, I figured it out. The sitting mom had wooden legs and was real above the waist, and
the one I had first seen had real legs but was a mannequin's
dummy from above her hips to her neck. They couldn't possibly get two heads, so they taxidermed one and carved a
dummy for the other, and then, I guessed, they could mix and
match the pieces back and forth. Where the extra hands came
from I didn't know.

At the time I also didn't know about the Rumbaugh history
with Peter and Hermann and the rest of them. I just knew I
had what my mother called the "love curse," and knew I was
drawn to wanting to keep her forever the way Ab and Dolph
kept their mother.

Then I felt playful again. "Mrs. Rumbaugh," I shouted out
from one doll to the other. "Do you have my scarf?"

"Yes," I replied to myself.

"Well, if you return it," I said, "I'll knit you your own."

I was so involved in this family conversation that I didn't
hear my mother open the pharmacy door.

"Ivy!" she suddenly called out from below. "Ivy, is that you up there?"

"Yes!" I yelled back, startled, but relieved that it was my mom. "Come see what I've found."

She pounded up the stairs and into the room before I could warn her.

"I knew something was wrong," she said breathlessly, wrapping her arms around me. "I woke with a start and kept calling on the phone, and when there was no answer my blood froze."

"I'm fine," I said. "I just got carried away playing with some new dolls."

"What do you mean?" she asked slowly, staring into my eyes. But I was sure she already knew.

"A second mother," I whispered, and turned her toward the table. "Now I know what you meant when you asked how many Mrs. Rumbaughs I had seen."

She made a disgusted face. "Oh, I'm so sorry you had to see this. I kept telling the boys that sooner or later you'd bump into her. Guess I should have warned you. *Duo non possunt in solido unam rem possidere*: 'Two cannot possess one thing each in entirety.' "

"They sawed her in half," I said.

She wrinkled up her nose. "I honestly don't want to know the gory details," she said. "The first time I saw this second one it nearly killed me. I had to turn off a water valve in the bathroom up here. There was a leak, and it was dripping through the ceiling. The boys were out somewhere so I just scampered up here as fast as I could and, good Lord, she was sitting here but with a head half molded, like something in a wax museum that had partially melted. It was gruesome— well, anyway I just screamed, and then I still had to pull myself together and turn off the water valve. For some reason I ran down to the other apartment, and there was the standing mother with the real head on. Lord, I screamed even louder. I think that was the first time I realized they had identical apartments. They bought two of everything alike—lamps, ashtrays, pictures, rugs, chairs. Even now the grocer brings two boxes of identical food. If one shops for clothes or shoes he always buys a second set. So it made sense then that they had two mothers preserved, one for each of them. Only, as I'm sure you figured out, there is just one real head. But I know they swap the real head day by day, because they told me.

"When I was working below in the pharmacy, I could hear the boys roll them both around up here, and they do talk to them. I wouldn't say they have long conversations, but they do have doll-talk kinds of conversations, like 'Would you like a drink?' and 'Did you have a nice day today?' Things along those lines. Nothing freakish. All very typical, except of course, that she is dead and somehow split in half. Believe me, it was good that I left the pharmacy and took a job in Greensburg."

"Oh," I cried out. "I almost forgot. They've been robbed. Someone broke into the drug cage. Should we call the police?"

"No," my mother said, wagging her finger back and forth. "The boys never want the police involved, as you can well understand." She nodded toward the mom. "Let's just lock up the place and go."

That made sense. "Meet you at the front door," I said, and bolted down the stairs all the way to the basement. I put the mother's head back in the cabinet just the way I found it. I didn't want the Twins to know what I had discovered. It didn't seem right to know something about them they wanted to keep a secret. And it would be rude, too, as if I came over while they were away and played with their toys.

I met Mom back up by the entrance. We jerked the front door closed, and it locked properly.

"It's that drug addict again," she said angrily. "I'm sure of it. He's picked the lock before. I told those boys to get a better lock, but they are so darn cheap."

Mom and I didn't talk much after we got home. She was tired and took her medicine, then went to bed. I crawled in next to her and listened to her breathing until she had fallen asleep. Then gently I touched her head and face, her shoulders, her arms and belly, her legs, and down to her feet. She was all there. All mine. And I loved every bit of her.

"Sleep tight," I whispered as if she were my big doll, then snuggled up beside her. I slept so well that night.

AN AWAKENING

 And it is as if I slept peacefully all the way until my mother spoke to me on my sixteenth birthday.

After that day I never looked at the Rumbaugh twins the same again. I didn't think of them as evil, just peculiar—as I said earlier—they were idiosyncratic variations within a breed. Still, all of the Rumbaugh history and this evidence of their blood-cursed relationship with their mother and mine did affect me. I never looked at myself the same again either. I had to admit, I was one of them through and through, and I had the evidence to back it up—it was in my genes. One of them was my father, and I resented that because it meant I wasn't entirely her duplicate—a perfect little *mini-Mom*. Of course I had known all along I had a father, but since I didn't know who he was, I didn't consider the shadow of his presence within me.

But now I did. And which shadow was it? It could have

been *either* of them. And I knew it would always bother me if I didn't find out which one. Not knowing would be worse than knowing. Mom couldn't get a straight answer out of them, so now it was my turn to "clear up a few things," as she said.

So when Mom went to work that following Monday, I did as I had when I was seven. I marched right over to the pharmacy. I opened the door and went downstairs into the taxidermy room, where I knew they would be.

I put my hands on my hips and said, "I need to have a serious talk with you two."

I looked over at Dolph, who was arranging THE PICTURE OF DORIAN GRAY, where a skunk in a tuxedo and top hat was staring bug-eyed at the pickled, wrinkled face of a decaying skunk mounted within a little golden picture frame.

"Yes," he said, and looked up at me.

Ab, who always did the lettering, was putting the title on the frame with a calligraphy brush and gold paint. He stopped in the middle of the G and looked over at Dolph.

"I need to know which one of you is my father," I said directly. There was no other way to say it but to blurt it out.

"Well, let's not be hasty here," Dolph said, looking as startled as when I had announced that the bear in the basement was their mother. "Slow down for a moment. Your mom told us she told you what all she knows, and we think it's time you know some things from our vantage point."

"No," I said. "This isn't about you! Now tell me, is it you?"

I pointed at Ab. "Or you?" I pointed at Dolph. "I want to know."

"We'll get to the father part," Dolph said, gesturing with his red hands for me to calm down, "but first just realize it's not an easy question to ask because in a way we are both your father—in a way you have to think of us as one person."

"I don't know what you mean," I said, suddenly stumped. In my mind I had thought one of them would just step forward and confess, but now they'd added a new twist I hadn't anticipated, and I was taken aback.

"Being a twin is both spiritual and physical," Ab said. "When Father had us adopted by those eugenics people, being a twin was a blessing. I was unhappy, but I knew what was going on inside of Dolph. I could *feel* what he was about. We liked the same food, and what he ate I could taste in my own mouth as he could with mine. We had toothaches at the same time. Sang the same songs. Had the same favorite colors. Same handwriting. Same grades in school. Same dreams. Same pets. Same names for the pets. I tell you, it was a comfort having him so vivid inside of me. And because it was my preoccupation to stay in tune with him like he was my shadow, my adoptive parents got angry with me for being so distant with them. One day they came to me wringing their hands and wiping kerchiefs across their faces and saying they had bad, bad news, that Dolph had died in a terrible mining accident. At first the tears shot out of my eyes, and then I just stood motionless and the next thing I knew I felt his arms wrapped around me, and so I knew he was warm still. It was as if we were one person and I could feel him next to me as sure as my heart is beating. *Not true!* I spit back at them. *You're lying. You just want him to go out of me, but all the lights in Pittsburgh will go out before he ever will.* I think that's when they lost interest in me, which was fine because I could just think more about Dolph. I always knew Mother would come get me, and of course she did.

"The eugenicists were wrong," Ab said. "It's not that certain genes are superior. All that selective breeding nonsense is rubbish. But twins *do* have a mysterious genetic bond. How twins can be so alike while being so far apart is the biggest challenge facing science. If all people are unique, how is it that we are so alike? Well, it means that there is something in the *genes* that controls behavior."

"Yes," Dolph said, stepping in. "We're the guinea pigs of the human race. First we were part of the eugenics study, then later we did the Minnesota study."

"What's that?" I asked.

"Another attempt to prove a point," Dolph said scornfully. "All the eugenics and Nazi hooey about Nordic and Aryan genes rising to the top of the food chain was wrong, but they were right in thinking that genes determine who we are more than our upbringing. The Minnesota study contacted us for their separated twin research on nonverbal communication and behavior similarities, but we declined to go—as if we could just close the store and go up and be lab chimps for a week. So they came here and gave us a bunch of tests and physical exams and asked about a million questions."

"And they didn't give us no answers," Ab said.

"But they did say we were not a good sample," Dolph added, "because we've lived together so long we may have just imitated each other from proximity."

"But it's more than that," Ab said. "When we were apart, we were more in harmony than we are now. Now we argue. Then, we only wanted to be like each other."

"True," Dolph said. "Being a twin can be more of a curse than *the family curse*. Think about it," he said directly to me. "We can't feel without the other one of us feeling the same. We can't laugh without the other having a tickle. We can't have pain without pain in the other. Anger begets anger. Desire, desire. If I take a drug, he too feels the results."

"Think of the burden of being cursed with a double," Ab said. "You haven't a life of your own—no thought, no pain, no love, no secret is safe between us. We know the insides of each other maybe better than we know ourselves. There are times when I ask, how does Dolph feel today? And the answer is often clearer than if I asked myself how I felt. Some days we don't even have to talk. We can just mind-read each other."

"Do you feel sorry for nontwins?" I asked.

"Yes and no," Dolph said, dropping his voice down low.

"It's like having an extra conscience, and there is a guilt, too. The guilt of knowing I'd never be free to fully be myself unless he died." He pointed at Ab.

"Or *he* died!" Ab pointed back.

"Until then, we live only half lives," Dolph said.

"And so that struggle to be alone," Ab continued, "to be just one individual self, is akin to some desire to murder the other. I'm telling you, it's not healthy. He's both jailer and companion. I could kill him at times."

Dolph smiled. "We take turns at feeling that," he said.

"We've worked so hard to just be ourselves we don't pay attention to what everyone else thinks," said Ab. "You must draw a bold line between who you are and what you do. If you sit around all day arm-wrestling with yourself about what you *should* be interested in and what you *should* say and how you *should* behave, then you're going to wear yourself down to nothing. You'll be as worthless as spit."

"He's right," Dolph said. "We disagree on a lot, but not on this. You have to live your life from the inside out, not from the outside in."

"What about me?" I asked. "After what Mom told me, I'm beginning to feel like two people. One of me is just playing out my heredity, and the other me is some thinking person who wants to forget about who I am on the inside and just do anything I please."

"You are different from us," said Dolph. "But your Rumbaugh affliction is like a twin self, and the older you become the stronger you'll find the fight between who you are and what you want to be."

"But I'm so upset," I said. "I never used to question any of this, and now that's all I do."

"You'll adjust," Ab said. "You'll find a way to just be yourself and drop all the questioning."

"But I'm not sure I want to be who I am," I said. "I'd like to become something else. Something I *do* invent."

"Hide the truth of who you are and you'll live a fiction," Dolph cautioned. "This is what most people want. A life made to fit a mold instead of a life that breaks it. That's why we live in the shadows."

"People don't always like us," Ab said.

"They find us odd," said Dolph.

"We *are* odd," Ab said irritably, "but that's not what I mean. I mean that we threaten them because we are so alike. Everyone believes that they are individuals and that their lives have been shaped through their experiences. But that's a charade, and they know it when they take one look at us because we are who we are through our genes. They believe in nurture, but we represent nature, and for most people nature is untamed and primitive and too dark and unpredictable. We live out our lives as the actors in a genetic script—that's nature's path."

"Think of it this way," said Dolph. "If you had to choose between being bullied around by your genes or bullied around by your environment, what would you do?"

I hesitated for a bit, thinking about the question. Neither choice seemed quite right. But they were too eager to allow me time to answer.

Dolph jumped right back in. "I would choose genes one hundred percent of the time. At least I'd be self-determined instead of having who I am be beaten into me by someone else."

"What about free will?" I asked.

"A sham," Dolph said emphatically and scoffed. "Free will is just a conscious struggle to manipulate your own destiny—the destiny that you end up fulfilling despite all the fussing and fighting with yourself. So you might as well let free will go the way of the dinosaur and just develop into who you are."

"And how do you know who you are?" I asked.

"By doing precisely what you feel like doing, and once you've done it then you have the concrete evidence in hand."

"Mother always called it *bliss*," Ab said. "She always said there was more intelligence in a drop of blood than in your entire brain."

"Said she never saw a person whose brain didn't get in the way of their behavior," said Dolph. "And I tend to agree with her."

"We fully believe in it," Ab said.

"But I'm not that way," I protested. "My brain is not in the way of my behavior."

"Exactly," Dolph said. "Because look at you. You're under the curse. You're part of this place. You can't leave. You love your mother like we do. Like all us Rumbaughs do. You'll never go away. That's a fact. You can't get away from who you are, from your bloodline."

"I can," I said defiantly. "And I will."

"Be careful," Ab said. "It's more than a curse. It's science. It's in your blood; the curse is part of your biology. Some people like hard work and it's passed on through the family. It's in the blood. Some people all have blond hair. That's passed along in the blood. Some people have asthma and so do their kids, so you know it runs in the family. So why can't a curse run through a family? The truth is that behavior is passed along through our genes, too."

"I don't know if that is totally true," I said.

"In your blood flows a bounden duty," Dolph said solemnly. "You can feel that it is up to you to pass on the curse of mother love."

"That's right," Ab said, reaching out to hold my arm. "You are the next generation."

"I thought your mother wanted to stop all this," I said, stepping away. "Isn't that why she kept you from getting married and having children? But didn't one of you have me?"

"Mother was wrong," Ab said. "She—"

They had taken over my conversation once already, but I wasn't about to let them do it again.

"You've made this all about you," I replied severely, "except for when it comes to owning up to the truth. So which of you is my father? It seems animals know more about their origins than I do."

Ab looked at Dolph, who in turn looked at Ab. A moment passed and they nodded toward each other, then both turned toward me.

"We'll get to that answer in a minute," Ab said. "But first we want to say something. We've been thinking about this for a long while, and we think that right now is the best time to bring it up."

"What's that?" I asked, stunned that there could be anything more important to discuss than who my father was.

"We want to offer you a full one-third ownership of the pharmacy and building," Dolph said. "To make you a partner. But in order for us to do so, you have to not leave here and go to college like your mother wants."

"You still haven't answered my question," I said, determined to press the issue. "I still need to know which one of you is my father."

"It doesn't matter which one of us it is," Dolph stammered. "We both planned it. We both have the same genes. We're the same. But just one of us could do it, and that was decided only with a coin toss."

"A coin toss?" I repeated loudly, and I could feel my blood rising in anger. "A coin toss?"

"Yes," said Ab, and poked himself in the chest. "I was heads and he was tails."

"So who won?" I asked.

Ab turned toward Dolph. A moment passed. As they read each other's minds, they shook their heads back and forth like a pitcher shaking off the sign from a catcher.

"Just call it a tie," Dolph said, breaking the silence. "And leave well enough alone."

"I need to know," I said. "It wasn't important before, but it has become important. If you won't tell me, then just show me. Pull down your pants and show me which one of you has the *A*."

They stepped back, and simultaneously their hands clutched their belt buckles. "We can't do that! Just think of both of us as your father," Ab said, rocking back and forth on the balls of his feet. "It's better left this way."

I was furious. "Then it's better I *left* this way," I shouted, and pointed toward the door. I grabbed my purse and marched right out.

"What about your taxidermy projects?" Dolph called out.

"That's over," I hollered back.

"What about preparing for your mother?"

Anger is a curse of an entirely different source. In a court of law they say: *Ira furor brevis est*: "Anger is a brief insanity." As I doubled-timed it up the steps, I felt insane.

When I reached the top, I turned around. "You know," I shouted angrily down into the basement hole, "it wouldn't be so bad if you'd get out from inside yourselves and see what's going on in the real world!"

"Think about our business offer," one of them hollered back. "Just let the idea sink in a little bit."

Before he could say another word, I slammed the basement door. Too much had already *sunk* into me. I closed the hasp over the ring and snapped the padlock into place. I remember thinking, *Maybe now they can flip a coin and see who is going to taxiderm the other.*

4
THE OTHER ONE

—and if God choose,
I shall but love thee better after death.
—Elizabeth Barrett Browning

BIRTHDAYS

Of course my angry stunt did not kill the Twins. They forced the door open, but nothing could force me back to the pharmacy. And even though we lived across the street from each other, their schedules were so predictable that it was easy to avoid them. Occasionally, from our rooms, Mom and I would glimpse them dashing about behind their windows. Sometimes they paced rapidly back and forth, talking wildly with their hands. Sometimes their crooked outlines stared out at us from behind a curtain pulled aside, or in uneven slices from between the venetian blinds. They stood perfectly motionless for so long that I guessed it was not them at all but their mothers, which they wheeled into position to keep an eye on us while they worked down in their basement.

I had to prove to the Twins that I made my own decisions and that I wasn't some animal, or plant, that was predetermined to be one thing and one thing only. I had a will and a mind of my own and could carve out my own life and make my own decisions. I told myself the curse was as phony as the myth of Dracula. I laughed at the thought of placing a braid of garlic around my neck to keep vampires and Rumbaughs at bay. It was all a primitive superstition. I mocked it and felt better for being so smug. It seemed to me my anger was the antidote to the curse.

Yet I had my doubts.

I must have learned all I needed to learn about taxidermy, because my interest in it declined once I stayed away from the pharmacy. Instead, I volunteered to stay after school at the church and work with Sister Nancy in their day-care program. It was good to put all my attention into something that was alive instead of constantly trying to enliven the dead. No longer did I look at lifeless creatures and wonder what natural pose I'd have to force onto their stiff bones and tendons, or what clothes and cosmetics they needed to look authentic, or what theatrical background I might paint for their species habitat. I began to enjoy them as living things that were more fun in motion than trapped inside a glass case. And when Mom came home after work, we ended up cooking, and chatting, and reading, and just being around each other in the most everyday sort of ways.

It was not the extraordinary events that drew me closer to my mother but the mundane. The constant pace of our lives, the comfort of our habits encouraged my love for her. It was a faithful love, and yet my fear of her death persisted, so that loving her and fearing her loss were always disturbingly together in the same thought. They were twin sensations, which I came to understand were more commanding than the living Twins across the street.

This entwined love and fear is why her birthday, which should have been a time of celebration, was always an uneasy reminder of her mortality. Her birthday was in January—a barren, icy month—and for weeks leading up to it I was always conflicted because I had to celebrate a day that announced she was one year closer to death. But my last semester of high school she decided that we would shake off the cold weather and take a vacation to celebrate her birthday in the Caribbean—at a nature preserve where we could live in a tent close to the sea. She was aware that in the fall I would be going off to Seton Hill to study religion as I had promised her, and I know she wanted to do something memorable with me before inching me out of the nest.

A few days before her birthday we were picked up by a shuttle service and driven to the airport. What I thought would simply be a trip where we would relax, celebrate her birthday, and escape the cold turned into a test of wills between the love curse and myself. I should have seen this clash coming, but I didn't.

After a few blissful days on the island, I suddenly began to think that if I changed my environment I could change who I was. This idea wasn't something unheard of, but when it just popped into my head like an unexpected guest, it got my attention. Perhaps, I thought, living in that old town, in that old hotel across from the crazy old Twins, was filling me with some old curse and all I had to do was move away and find some fresh air and warm water and beautiful gardens and I could be reborn in some tropical Eden without the burden of that curse haunting me day and night, so that when I looked at my mother I would feel only love without the fear.

I was still young and naïve enough to think disregarding my past was an option. I thought that I could will myself into becoming another person and that all I needed was a change of scenery in order to have a change of heart. It's not that I was infected with a curse, I thought, but the curse was an affliction upon me, and all I had to do was choose to turn my back and walk away from it.

In her own way, Mom was doing the same thing. She was tired of her work and the small town and the Twins, and she just wanted a break from it all, too. And she got it. Overnight we were wearing bathing suits and living in a tent on a sandy beach. After those first few days of pure happiness, I was convinced that changing myself was absolutely possible. The curse seemed to evaporate under the sun, and I remained a cheery teenage girl who wanted her mother to be wonderfully happy on her birthday. The more I thought like this the happier I became.

All Mom wanted as a gift from me was for us to be normal. So on the night of her birthday, I cooked snapper on a camp stove under the stars. Then I made her close her eyes and I led her down the beach.

"No peeking," I said, leading the way to a huge cake I had earlier built out of sand. I had stuck candles all over it.

"One more minute," I said to her, and quickly lit the candles. "Okay, now open your eyes," I shouted, and when she did I sang "Happy Birthday" and we danced in each other's arms in the candlelight as small waves patted the shore. We were surrounded by nature and animals, and even without saying so to each other we felt we had become a part of the world, instead of being apart from the world.

It was a marvelous celebration. She looked so healthy. So happy. So young. And my love for her felt entirely free from my fear of her death. It was heavenly. I didn't think of home, or school, or the pharmacy. She was joyful and so I was joyful. And when I suddenly realized just how vastly the change in scenery had affected me, it seemed there was a way to escape my old self forever and be this happy all the time, and in an instant the trip was all about me again.

The next day we were side by side on a hammock reading beach novels when I lowered my book and blurted out, "Did we take this vacation because you knew a change of scenery would do me good?"

She smiled. "A change of scenery does everybody good," she replied.

"Then," I reasoned, "if we moved from Mount Pleasant, maybe we'd be happy like this all the time?"

"I'm already happy with you all the time," Mom said, and kissed me.

"I think a move would be a good idea," I continued.

"After you finish college," she replied with some gravity.

"I don't want to wait that long," I said. "Let's just do it now."

"You know we *have* to stay," she said, referring to my promise to Sister Nancy that I'd study religion. "Then I can think about taking a different job and we can move out of town. I agree that the place has put a damper on us."

"Yes," I said with the enthusiasm of a new discovery. "Because if we move I can get away from the curse for good. I can love you without always thinking I'm going to lose you. And you can love me without thinking there is something wrong inside me, like Mrs. Rumbaugh always thought there was something wrong with the Twins. All we have to do is move. It's as simple as that."

"I agree that a change of scenery is helpful. But I also think that if you really want to change, you will," she said slowly, deliberately. "You can change at any time. You can't give up hope that you'll lick that curse." She reached out and touched me, and I held her hand as her strength and hope became my strength and hope.

"Yes," I said quietly. "I can change."

"See how easy it is to work out a problem when you talk about it?" she said.

"A worry shared is a worry halved," I recited. "That's what they say back at the pharmacy."

"The real curse is having to hang around with a bunch of Rumbaughs," Mom said jokingly. "Get rid of them and you'll be fine."

I laughed because she laughed. It was as simple as that—get rid of them and get rid of the curse. It seemed too good to be true.

The next day I was sitting on the same beach staring at her. Her body was so young and firm, and after the days of sun she looked radiant while collecting shells and pieces of beach glass and bird feathers. She could live forever, I thought, as she waded out into knee-deep water that was patchy with white sand and coral heads. The more I watched her the more I thought of our bright future together. *Forever*—it was a word with an endless echo.

Suddenly she cried out in pain. I jumped up and ran down to the water's edge as she hobbled toward the shore. My heart raced.

"I've stepped on something sharp," she called out.

"What happened?" I asked as I held her arm and steadied her.

"A sea urchin," she said, and winced.

We crossed the sand and dropped down beneath the shade of a coconut palm. I lifted her foot and looked at the sole.

There were about a dozen black urchin spines snapped off inside her heel. "Did you pack tweezers?" I asked.

"Yes," she said as I stood up. "And bring a candle and matches, too. I read somewhere that you have to drip hot wax on the spines to draw them up above the surface of the skin so you can get a grip on them."

I dashed over to the tent and quickly sorted through our little first-aid kit for the tweezers and gauze. The extra birthday candles and matches were on a wooden pallet we used as a deck.

When I returned I lit a candle.

"This may hurt," I said.

"I don't like pain," she warned me, and rolled over onto her stomach with her foot upturned, "but do what you have to do to get them out." Then she buried her face into her crossed arms.

I dripped the hot wax over the broken ends of the spines. When the wax cooled I carefully peeled some away with the edge of the tweezers until I found where just the head of a dark spine had risen above the surface. With the tweezers I deftly gripped it, then gingerly pulled it out. A drop of blood seeped up behind it. "One down," I said to her, and dabbed at the blood with a tissue.

Methodically I tracked down each spine. My gift of focus was on her. I wanted to fix her. To have her be as good as new. To make all her pain go away. To have her back the way she was—sunning and prancing along the beach without a care in the world.

After I removed the last spine, she sighed and the pooled blood on her heel slipped down her oily calf.

And in my own way I slipped, too. It was seeing that red

streak that caused me to recall something the Twins had drilled into me over and over as we worked in the taxidermy shop. "A person's blood is the key to their future," Ab lectured. "One drop and everything will be revealed, just like opening a book. Whoever examines your blood will know your eye color, will know if you stutter, or if you are left-handed or right-. They'll know if you wear glasses and how tall you are. They'll know your IQ and what medications you should be taking and just how much you love your mother. In one strand of DNA they'll find out things about you that you don't even know about yourself. The genetic trail doesn't lie," he stressed. "The mind may choose to ignore science, but science never ignores the mind."

I didn't want to recall the Twins. But it was too late. I had opened the door to my past, and in that moment everything snapped back to how I was. I looked up for a moment at the ocean and the sand and the trees, and suddenly all the beauty around me was just as counterfeit as the belief that I was free to steer my own future. That wretched curse surfaced like a bloated corpse, and I could feel the coldness of my mother's death in my hands while my fears ran through me like a predator tracking down whatever hope I sheltered.

My fingers began to shake. As I examined her foot one last time, the tweezers scraped across the tiny cuts on her skin, and she trembled as the blood continued to run down her leg.

"Are you okay?" she asked.

"Yes," I said, but I wasn't.

I didn't have the heart to tell her I had reverted for the worse. Her hope had been my hope. The curse may have taken my hope away, but I could not be a curse to her.

Carefully, I wrapped her foot with gauze. Afterward I stood over her and reached down for her hand.

"It will be sore for a little bit," I cautioned. "But I'm sure I got them all out."

"You are a love," she said, and kissed me. She was fine, but I wasn't. I helped her over to the tent and propped her foot up on a pillow and got her a cold drink and a magazine.

Ab and Dolph had secrets they could not share with the world, but at least they had each other. As I sat by my mother's side, the loneliness I felt from not sharing my despair was defeating. My secrets were a cage visible only to me. I was trapped with knowing that fearing my mother's death was the same as predicting her death. I didn't know when it would happen, or how. But it would. Warning her would serve no purpose because there was no hiding from the inevitable.

Three days later we returned to Mount Pleasant. It was just as cold and dreary as when we had left. After my first day back at school, I hurried home to our rooms. I peeked out from behind the curtains and watched the Twins come and go. It seemed that I was always engaged in pushing them away or being pulled toward them. Either way, something within me was not quite settled.

FAST FORWARD

Who you think you are is only your personal opinion. And if it is only through our blood that the truth can be fully understood, as Ab and Dolph would say, then the facts of what actually happens in a story are always so much more accurate than how it is told.

So this is what happened next.

In all the years I had known the Twins they had never come to visit us in the Kelly Hotel. To my knowledge they had never entered the lobby. But as the summer passed and I prepared to leave for college for my calling into the church, they were compelled to come speak to me.

Mom had stayed after Mass to try out for the choir. I knew she was beginning to look for ways to fill her time once I had moved out. I was home when the Twins knocked at our door. I answered. It had been raining hard, and they were as soaking wet as two old otters. They had walked down from the Lutheran church without an umbrella.

I made them stand in the hall.

"Have you thought about our offer?" one of the Twins immediately asked in a sharp voice, picking right up where we'd left off when last we spoke over a year ago.

He caught me by surprise. "I'm not sure what you mean," I replied.

"A third of the pharmacy, like Dolph and I said," Ab blurted out. "You can still have it."

"But I don't want any part of the pharmacy," I said adamantly.

"It would be to your advantage to take it," Dolph said.

I repeated to them what I had promised my mother—that I was going to college, and that I was going to board at Seton Hill, then enter the church and never return. The more mute they remained the more I kept repeating my plans until they literally looked like two wet hens, nearsighted and plucked from worry. I was merciless. They were beaten down, but not defeated.

"Well, you'll be back," Ab predicted. "Running off won't work."

"It's your destiny," Dolph insisted. "You can't just leave your mother like this."

"It's not right," said Ab. "And your affliction won't stand for it. We're warning you. Bad things will happen."

"We tried to leave once," Dolph said in a whisper. "Tried to make a break for a normal life. But we had to return."

"It wasn't good for Mother," Ab added. "We hid out in

Youngstown for a month, and it put her in bad health. Nearly killed her. We returned just in time to save her."

"I'll be fine, and so will Mother," I said firmly. "I'm moving on." And what I said next was calculated to set them into a fury. "Free will trumps the genetic curse," I said defiantly.

"You can't possibly believe that!" Ab sputtered, shocked at the thought. "Free will is just stimulus–response. You think because you are hungry and seek food you are free? That's biology, not *brains*."

"I really don't want to discuss this anymore," I said. "I'm going to close the door now. I have to get ready to leave."

Dolph became very agitated. "Yes, yes," he said nervously. "I can see you are determined to move on."

"Yes," Ab said hastily. "Best wishes." He reached into his pocket and pulled a hundred dollars from his money clip. Dolph did exactly the same.

"Thank you," I replied as they pressed the bills into my hand. "This is very kind of you."

"One final thing," Dolph said. "Just remember that we love your mother, too."

"But I love her more," I replied.

"We don't want anything to happen to her," Ab said, pleading.

"She'll be fine," I said emphatically.

They stood there, shoulders turned down like bent coat hangers beneath the soggy weight of their thick wool coats, and then they slogged away, leaving a puddle behind.

As they departed, their surrender troubled me. I knew they couldn't predict the future, but their warning about Mother made me nervous because their concerns were so similar to my own.

I took a small suitcase down from the closet. My entrance interview included a one-night orientation. I neatly folded up all the clothes I thought I needed, then organized my cosmetics and toiletries. I was set.

When Mom came home I told her the Twins had come up to the apartment.

"Did they touch you?" was the first question she asked. It was a very odd question, but because I had so much on my mind I let it pass, just like the time she'd asked me how many Mrs. Rumbaughs I had seen.

I laughed nervously. "Just relax," I replied. "I told them I was going to Seton Hill, and they wished me luck and gave me money."

"They've been very nervous about you going away," she said. "I just don't want them stirring up any trouble."

I didn't tell her that the real trouble was already stirring up inside me. I couldn't. Ever since the vacation I had hid my fears from her. If I had any worries with the curse, I passed them off as worries over my calling.

"Please call Sister Nancy and tell her I'll meet her at the interview." I insisted. It made me feel better to make plans I could count on rather than dwell on premonitions.

My mother picked up the phone. She confirmed everything.

The following morning I went with my mother on the bus into Greensburg. I didn't talk much because I was afraid my own words would influence me in the wrong way. After we got off at the stop next to the courthouse, Mom put me into a taxi.

"You be careful up at school tonight," she said. "I don't know what I'd do without you."

I leaned forward and put my head on her shoulder. "I know exactly what I'd do with you," I said slyly.

"Shhh," she said. "Don't talk like that. You're getting ready to go study religion."

"I thought religion was all about honesty," I replied.

"Don't mix up honesty and piety," she advised. "In the Catholic Church that's always been a good way to lose your head."

When she said the word *head*, we both laughed. It was a Rumbaugh joke between us, and the laughter cleared the air of the tension gathered from me moving away.

She gave me a kiss. "Remember, you are doing the right thing."

I smiled tightly and nodded in agreement. That was the best I could do. As the cab pulled away from the curb, I blew her a kiss. She blew a kiss in return. It was like we were playing dolls with each other.

There are times when questioning the future is a distraction from fully entering the present. While I had my entrance interview with a lovely lady, Mrs. Burnes, who did everything to make me feel welcome and comfortable, my mind was elsewhere. I was thinking of the first time I saw Mrs. Rumbaugh in the basement, because that was when I began to anticipate and prepare for my mother's death. Sometimes an inner instinct, a gut feeling for something is just as certain as the facts. Facts may be needed to convince other people about what might or might not happen. But I needed to convince only myself, and my gut instinct was triumphant. It would kill my mother if I didn't go to Seton Hill. It would kill her if I went. I was stuck between these two thoughts as if I were stuck between Ab and Dolph. There was nothing to do but play out the hand I had been dealt.

I finished the interview as if I had been a puppet—polite, poised, and not a word out of place. Mrs. Burnes asked me to step outside while she and Sister Nancy spoke privately. Perhaps they had detected something worrisome about me. Maybe they were just choosing my roommate for the evening. I'll never know.

There were a few other girls in the hallway. I didn't want to make small talk, so instead of waiting I took a stroll around the campus. It had been founded on the crown of a hill that overlooked all of Greensburg. I drifted aimlessly along a path and found myself at the entrance to the nuns' burial ground. I cut diagonally across the grass rows, which were studded with a uniform grid of molded iron crosses. Where their flat black paint had ruptured, crusty blossoms of rust left red stains running down into the earth. I thought of my mother's upturned leg on the beach and the blood running into the sand. Landscape is always about mortality, and the red-streaked crosses looked like a defeated army of crusaders heading home. My hope to escape the curse had been defeated, too. I bent my head and said a prayer. It was the best I could do.

I turned toward the northeast and saw the granite dome of the courthouse, and in my mind I could lift it as if lifting the top of a teapot and peer down inside and watch as my mother sat at her courtroom station and recorded trials. Ab and Dolph had said that their separation as boys strengthened the unspoken depth of their bond. I understood what they meant. The farther they were from each other the more intense was their perception, as if distance only magnified their sensitivity. As I stared over at the dome, I seemed to be able to feel my mother inside of me, and yet it was I who came from within her, like a fetal spy sensing everything about her. For a moment I closed my eyes and imagined the heartbeat we shared. I was transfixed with this sanctuary of darkness when I received that final calling.

"Ivy!" the admissions officer, Mrs. Burnes, called out from her office window. Her voice was like a rope come to get me. She waved her hand over her head. Though she was far enough away to be the size of a mouse, the alarm in her clear voice was palpable. Fear stormed through me. In a few minutes Sister Nancy emerged from the ground-floor door, and as she ran toward me she called out my name, which was echoed again by Mrs. Burnes. My ears became so sharp then. It was as though I wasn't listening but sounds arrived from within me. Gravel crunched loudly beneath Sister's rubber-soled shoes. The wind slithered like snakes across the wet grass. Her wheezing was like curtains blowing through an open window.

"Ivy!" she panted, slowly growing closer so that I could read the hysteria in her face, and I knew then without having to be told what she was about to say, because as I turned away and looked out over the crosses toward the dome of the courthouse, I said it first to myself.

"Ivy!" Sister called. I turned toward her and watched her open mouth pull down like the Greek mask of tragedy. Behind her the weather had changed, and overhead the clouds looked like the destruction of an ancient city, with the white cumulus pillars tumbling unsteadily against a smoky sky.

Finally, she reached me, but she was too exhausted to speak. She pressed her hand against my shoulder and bent over. She drew in a halting set of breaths before lifting her head. But my words arrived first.

"My mother is dead," I said flatly, as if they were the most certain words I had ever spoken. And then everything before me vanished. I passed out.

An ambulance must have been called. I was carted off. Examinations were performed. But I remember nothing of this.

I woke up in the same hospital where my mother was but on a different floor. I was in the emergency room, and she was in the morgue. Ab and Dolph were sitting next to me.

"Ivy," they said conspiratorially when I opened my eyes and turned my head toward them. "We have to act quickly."

I knew what he meant. I was prepared for this moment. The curse had trained me well. I slid my legs out from under the blanket and stood up. And though I was in shock, I walked as if following a marked path through fog. The Twins held my hands, and together we padded down the hall and out the door. They had already called Mr. Sweet at the funeral home. He had worked with Ab and Dolph on their mother and would manage my mother's release from the hospital and deliver her to us as soon as we were ready.

Even though Ab and Dolph had warned me not to leave my mother, it is impossible for me to connect her death to the curse. Simply, she had gone down to Tommy's Book Shelf to buy me a book to mark the beginning of my college career when the accident happened. After all the crime she witnessed in her work, all the hate and wickedness, she died so innocently. She was walking back up Pennsylvania Avenue and was next to the courthouse when a delivery truck backfired. It startled her, and she caught a heel on a metal service grate, pitched headfirst, and hit awkwardly against the building's brass standpipe. She must have known she couldn't get her hand ahead of her face to brace her fall, so instead she turned her face away but hit her temple flush on the raised knuckle of a brass bolt. She fractured her skull. She had a brain hemorrhage and was dead by the time Mrs. Burnes had hollered my name from her office window. Altogether I spent only about four hours at the college. Once my mother died, the curse fully occupied the space she'd left behind, and whatever religious goals I had gave way to my adoration of her.

When Ab and Dolph and I left the hospital, we drove toward the pharmacy to prepare for her.

"We can help," they said, and without another word spoken I knew what they meant. We could manage her, as Ab and Dolph had done with their mother, in a traditional way, by skinning her and removing the organs and flesh and then preserving the skin with a better generation of chemicals that would leave her more supple and lifelike, unlike Mrs. Rumbaugh, who had dried out and turned nut-brown over the years. Or we could stuff her and coat her with a thin veneer of tinted resin to seal out the air while securing her true color.

The decision really hinged on whether I wanted to preserve her body entirely, as done with big game, or create an artificial model, which was what I had learned to do with large fish. I wanted both. I wanted some part of her to touch that was real, not just a resin model. Like the faithful, I wanted to touch something sacred—a saint's lock of hair, a bone, a withered face. To touch what is human, and to feel human in response, was what I craved. So I decided to keep her hands. It seemed a traditional choice—and they are so elegant.

"I have it figured out," I quietly said to the Twins.

"Any way you want. Right, Dolph?" Ab replied.

"Anything at all," said Dolph, who reached up from the backseat and put his fingers on my shoulder.

"How long will Mr. Sweet give us with the body?" I asked.

"Before or after embalming?" he replied.

"Before," I said. "I don't want any marks. I want to make a mold." They knew exactly what technique I meant to apply.

While I waited at the pharmacy with Dolph, Ab went to purchase the supplies. As soon as he returned with the five-gallon buckets of mold-grade latex and a plastic liner for a bathtub, he called Mr. Sweet. It didn't take him long to arrive.

Mother wasn't badly hurt, so we didn't have to worry much about rebuilding any of her bone structure. I gave her a kiss, whispered the few things I needed to say into her ear, and then got busy. First, we lifted her into the tub and coated her skin with Vaseline so the latex wouldn't stick.

The five-gallon bucket was too heavy for me to lift, so I used a quart measuring cup to dip into the latex, then pour over her feet. Dolph watched to make sure I was following his directions. "Slowly," he cautioned, "or it bubbles up into a honeycomb. It's not hard to patch, but it will never look natural."

"Okay," I replied, and slowed down, trying in part to imagine I was icing a cake, but mostly I was turning over the word *natural*, which he had used to describe the effect we were trying to achieve. I did want her to look natural, exactly like she had while alive, rather than like some of the twinkle-eyed, stiff-furred, lacquer-lipped animals that every taxidermist had in his shop. I had given a lot of thought to the results I wanted. After making the life-size mold, we could release the body back to the funeral home. From the mold we could then make a positive image using more firm, "human"-grade latex,

which could be skin-tinted. I would add a jointed wire armature to the core so she could be manipulated into positions. I
could then paint her with an airbrush so she appeared real.
And if I wanted, I could make as many as I wished. But for
now, I just wanted one.

As we worked, we made sure the latex got all the way under
her outstretched arms and into the folds of skin and over her
face until she was fully submerged. Then we waited for it to
cure. It didn't take long.

We had an open casket at the viewing, and Mother looked
splendid. Mr. Sweet embalmed her after we returned her to the
funeral home. I picked out her clothing and did her hair and
makeup. She looked so young, almost like my twin. And with
a silk shawl draped across her middle, no one could notice her
missing hands, which I had kept for myself. Father Baumann
gave the funeral Mass, and Mother was buried in the Rumbaugh cemetery, in the exact spot she had shown me on my
birthday. Her death and burial had all happened so quickly.
Just some weather blowing through, she might have said.

UNFINISHED BUSINESS

After my mother's death, it rained for a long time and after a while a lush green moss like a rash of sadness settled over the town. Loud sounds dissolved quietly beneath the constant hiss of drizzle. The clouds paused above us as if they had indefinitely canceled their travels. The drip of water replaced the ticking of clocks.

At first I thought the weather so loved my mother that it draped over us like black bunting. But the lethargy has continued over Mount Pleasant, long past the etiquette for mourning. You can feel the town exhale as it slumps forward like something hungry and tired. It seems to be sadly weighing its worth, which is not much. The rain continues.

People are poor. Business is poor. And both are getting worse. Plans have been discussed to invigorate commerce and give Main Street a face-lift to restore its former glory. But there is no funding, and the town seems to be fighting for its life. The vital young people leave to make plans in new places, and those who stay seem to resent themselves. Without opportunities, the townies mill around and wish for things they want but will never have. They fight over the corpse of the place—gravediggers against vultures. Even crime is mismatched. It takes too much risk for too little reward.

However, the old people still stick together, steadfastly remaining to be buried where they had always planned. Each day the ones who are able inch down the wet sidewalk toward the pharmacy with a cane in one hand and an umbrella in the other. Their lives are propped up on medication like fake cowboy towns on movie sets. And for those who can't make it to the pharmacy, I deliver their prescriptions. I even pour them glasses of water. I read their mail out loud and feed their pets. I clean out their refrigerators and take out their trash. I wash their sheets and clip their nails. Many are so thin their skeletal postures are studies in how armatures should be constructed in taxidermed subjects. Sometimes, as I read to them, they stretch out on the couch and fall asleep. The overhead lights transform their thin, dried-out noses and shallow faces into sundials. They have so little time left. I can only wish that science will hurry up and discover ways to keep them alive, make them vital again and young with laughter. Ab was right; it is our job to help those who can't help themselves. That mission has now become my calling. To help and to offer hope to others. That's all I've ever really wanted to do.

Because Mother died of head trauma, there was nothing I

could do to help her. If she were diabetic, I would have given her a kidney. If she had leukemia, I would have hoped to be a perfect match. I would have given of myself whatever she needed. Now, I have to wait for science to provide the next step. I have saved her genetic material for the future. There are many things to fear about the science of cloning. We still have fetal attrition, tissue overgrowth, and poor survival after birth. But biotechnology is progressing; we are finding solutions. Already you can have your pet cloned for fifty thousand dollars. You can clone personal "savior babies," from which you can harvest your own stem cells for future illnesses. There are countries with advanced laboratories that are already working on crafting designer babies.

I can have Mother's genetic samples altered. She did always want to be taller, so that gene could be added. She could have better eyesight, a stronger memory, no freckles, more acumen for languages, a faster metabolism. When the time comes, there will be a lot of improvements to consider. However, I always found her interest in the weather charming, so I would leave that alone. Eventually her designed genetic material will be implanted into my egg, which first would have had my genetic material removed. Then my mother could become my baby. And someday, when I get old, I can become her baby. Then she will be mine. And I will be hers. We will take the men out of it altogether. It will be pure mother love. Just me and her and me and her forever.

Now when I look back on why I had the Rumbaugh curse, I

can see that I am the beginning of the future. In the past the mother love needed men for biological reasons. But no more. Science has caught up to our desires. The Rumbaugh women won't need them anymore. We'll store their necessary tissues in a genetic bank and be able just to keep to ourselves.

When I hold her hands and warm them with my own, I think about keeping my preserved mother close to me. I don't know why more people won't do it. I suppose they think it has to do with religion and respect for the dead—to allow their souls to rest in peace. But upon death the soul is instantly gone from the body and lofted toward the hall of judgment. No amount of prayers can ever reach the judges' ears to sway their considerations between heaven and hell because judgment takes place the second death occurs. We can really only hope that they made it to heaven, and if they went to hell, well then, the prayers are useless, unless you take the point of view that prayers are really a way that the living express their grief. In which case, prayers are very therapeutic.

But I don't need prayers because I have created heaven in my own home. Having my mother by my side is a comfort. I don't know why anyone would think that a three-dimensional image would be any different than a painted portrait, a home movie, or a recorded voice. It is no different than keeping your mother's jewelry, good china, and silver keepsakes. So having my mother to talk to, to dress, to move around and keep company is so uplifting.

She is a saint to me, a beautiful relic. She doesn't at all look like one of those grotesque European relics—a fragment of bone, or an eviscerated head secured in a glass-and-gold-filigreed box, or a lock of hair or decayed tooth. She looks beautiful. Hand-painted, and honestly, at first glance you would think she was alive. Her joints move back and forth just as I had imagined as a child. Each day I adjust her poses, and I often give her a window view so she can follow the weather. I can even detach limbs if need be, and put her in a special case and take her with me if I travel. I did not motorize her, but I have an office chair I can sit her in to wheel her from room to room. After all, she is a bit too heavy to carry.

For a lot of daughters, the dead mother is a moral curse judging each and every move they make. Nothing the daughter says, or does, or doesn't do is good enough or proper enough or wise enough or pleasing enough to the memory of the dead mother. But not for me. What kind of life could I lead if my mother existed only as idealized perfection lording over me? It would be as if I could never make any mistakes or have any faults that her memory wouldn't judge harshly. Instead of her memory being a comfort to me, it would be a haunting. That unforgiving attitude belongs to the gothic past. I prefer to think of my mother as a mother who has nurturing qualities and depth—a mother I could have a dialogue with, a mother who could disagree with me yet even in death would love me unconditionally no matter what I did.

But even unconditional love has its boundaries, so there are times when I don't tell my mother everything. Like Mrs. Rumbaugh, my mother did not want to advance the love curse to another generation. This creates a conundrum for me: Do I follow my mother's orders and never allow myself to be trapped into having the mercy sex she did? Or do I follow the curse that runs through my veins and have a baby? Sometimes I think if I had just done what my mother had done, she would still be alive. Had I carried out the Rumbaugh curse with Ab or Dolph, I would have had a baby and my mother and I and the baby would have lived together like three links of a chain, locked in our own impenetrable triangle. But instead I planned to go away, which threatened the logic of the curse and set into motion a series of tragic events.

Now I know what my mother meant when she asked if the Twins had "touched" me.

It was as if the curse had to get my mother out of the way so I would return to the Twins. Just as the boys couldn't carry on the curse until their mother died, I couldn't carry it on until mine died. She died so that the curse could live, and if I don't carry on the curse, she will have died in vain.

Recently I felt I had to honor her sacrifice. She always wanted to know which Twin she had slept with. She had called it her "unfinished business." Out of respect for her, I thought it was business that should be finished. I knew I would have to confront the Twins, and to give me courage I put her real hands deep into my overcoat pockets. Holding them was always a comfort.

I was working at the pharmacy now that I owned a third of

it, so I left the hotel and walked across the street. Ab and Dolph were sitting at the soda counter eating ice cream.

"So," I said, unleashing my plan, "which one of you is my father?"

"Not that again," one said impatiently, and slumped over his bowl.

"Come on," I said in a joking way. "Just stand up and pull down your pants. Let's get this over with."

"No," said the other, crossing his arms and stiffening his back.

"Never," his brother insisted, puffing himself up.

"Then let me put it to you this way," I said directly. "If I'm going to perpetuate the Rumbaugh curse, it should be with the one of you who is *not* my father."

Their eyes seemed to pulse like something electrical about to burn out. They turned and looked at each other for a moment and communicated in that silent way they did.

Finally, they reached some decision and faced me. "Okay," they said as one. "Pull the shades."

I did.

Then both of them stood up and slowly unbuckled their belts and tugged down their pants; then they lowered their boxer shorts just a bit. I walked around them, and to my surprise they both had red *A*'s on their *left* cheeks. I was stumped.

"Mother said there was only *one A*," I said. "It makes sense that the doctor would mark only one of you if he was trying to distinguish the difference. So what happened?"

"Your mother was wrong," one explained as they both

pulled their pants up. "The judge checked both Dolph and me, and we both had the letter scar, and on the left cheek."

"The doctor had marked me when I was a baby," said Dolph.

"But while we were separated as boys, I gave myself an *A* in order to feel closer to him," Ab said. "I cut myself with a razor."

"So my mother was wrong?" I pondered.

"Doubly so," replied Dolph. "She also made a mistake saying it was on the right side when it was on the left."

"Because of the mirror," added Ab, shaking his head. "She saw it *backward*."

At that moment I felt so sorry for her. I reached into my pockets and caressed her hands. I knew she would be so embarrassed by having made such a silly mistake. But I couldn't just stop.

"So whichever one of you did it, why didn't you marry her?" I asked.

The thought was incredible to them. "We couldn't marry your mother," Dolph explained. "We already have one."

"And then we have each other," Ab said, pointing to Dolph. "One of us couldn't get married. We can't split up."

"And," said Dolph, "you turned out to be a girl, which seemed all wrong."

"So," I asked again, "which of you is my father? I have to know, because if I'm going to carry on the curse, it can't be with him."

Dolph was defiant. "I'm not telling," he said.

"Then I'll flip a coin," I replied coolly. "Turnabout is fair play." I fished one out of my pocket. "You are heads," I said to Ab. "And you are tails," I said to Dolph.

I flipped the coin, caught it, and slapped it onto my forearm. "Heads it is," I announced. "Let's go, Ab." I pointed upstairs and grabbed his arm.

"I can't," he said, lowering his eyes and tugging against my grip. "I can't do it with you."

"Why?" I pressed.

"You know *why*," he stammered. He pointed at Dolph, who looked terrified. "You'll have to do it with him. It's his turn."

That was all I needed to know. Now I could go home and tell my mother it was Ab. It would be a comfort to her.

"Keep your pants on," I said to both of them, dropping Ab's arm and stepping away. "I just wanted to see which one of you it was." I thought they might be annoyed with me for pulling such a stunt, but they actually looked relieved.

From when I was a child, I had thought it would make a difference when I finally knew. I wanted to say "Father," but the word was surprisingly hollow after all the years of saying "Mother." Besides, he was just the Twin who won the coin toss.

"Remember, you are a Rumbaugh," Ab said. "It's in your blood to somehow pass it on."

"I will," I said. Then I hesitated for a moment, as if I needed to say something more, as if there was still an inchoate thought lurking inside me like a second curse that wanted to reveal itself now that the first had been put to rest. But no further thought came to mind.

"Good night," I said, feeling puzzled.

I turned and walked out of the store. I took another step, and then that inchoate thought turned out to be something after all—one curse had given birth to another. It bubbled up from the dark recesses of my mind and became perfectly clear. It would be easy enough. My mother had done so, and I was as much her as I was myself.

This thought stopped me in the middle of the street. I turned and looked back toward the pharmacy. The shades were pulled down. The Closed sign hung in the door. Then, from Dolph's second-floor parapet, I saw his pale arm reach out toward me and beckon me closer with his hand. Was he reading my mind? Did he too have second thoughts? Was he too now thinking of creating an heir to the curse? Was I to provide him with the same mercy my mother had provided his brother?

"Yes?" I called out. I took a step toward him and then another, as if I were a bride marching toward the altar.

The pull of the curse was in the palm of his hand. He was waving me toward him the way you wave a toy boat to shore. The current of the Rumbaugh curse tugged at me, and I could feel the desire of wanting a child to love me as much as I loved my mother. I didn't want to be alone forever. I wanted someone to hold my hand, too.

"What can I do for you?" I called out.

He leaned forward. "Say good night to your mother for me," he whispered in his sweet old voice, a voice that banished my previous thought back to the shadows of the unthinkable.

"And to yours," I replied warmly. Then he turned and opened the door into his sitting room. It was his night to have his mother's real head. Ab would not sleep well, but Dolph would sleep like a baby.

"Good night," I said behind him, then quickly crossed over into the Kelly Hotel. I took the elevator up to the third floor. I walked down the hall, removed my keys, and unlocked the door. I closed it behind me and twisted the knob on the dead bolt. Then I called out gently, "Don't worry, Mom. It's just me."